Waiting for Next Week

Waiting for Next Week

Michele Orwin

Henry Holt and Company
New York

Copyright © 1988 by Michele Orwin
All rights reserved, including the right to reproduce
this book or portions thereof in any form.
Published by Henry Holt and Company, Inc.,
115 West 18th Street, New York, New York 10011.
Published in Canada by Fitzhenry & Whiteside Limited,
195 Allstate Parkway, Markham, Ontario L3R 4T8.

Library of Congress Cataloging in Publication Data
Orwin, Michele.
Waiting for next week.
I. Title.
PS3565.R96W35   1988   813'.54   87-25125
ISBN 0-8050-0517-X

First Edition

This is a work of fiction.
Names, characters, places, and incidents
are either the product of the author's imagination
or are used fictitiously,
and any resemblance to actual persons,
living or dead, events, or locales,
is entirely coincidental.

Printed in the United States of America
10 9 8 7 6 5 4 3 2 1

ISBN 0-8050-0517-X

For Freddy

Acknowledgments

This book could not have been completed without the gentle guidance of N.D. and R.E.; the perceptive suggestions of Gail Hochman and Channa Taub; the thoughtful comments of Wanda Fries, Linda Greenwald, Valmai Howe, Martha Hughes, Joe Levine, Jeanne Mackin, Sue William Silverman, Norman Tamarkin, and Laura Tracy; the humor and wisdom of Seth and Carly Rosenberg; and the encouragement of my family and friends.

Childhood is the kingdom where nobody dies.
Nobody that matters, that is.

—Edna St. Vincent Millay

Waiting for Next Week

1

It was two days before Christmas and the air was so cold it hurt to be outside. The flashing billboard above the Dupont Circle metro station put the temperature at seventeen degrees. The windchill factor cut it down to ten below. Already the old Iranian woman hawking hats and gloves from her fold-out table was in business. The sidewalk sax player warmed up with "Satin Doll" and the music woke Captain Video, our neighborhood street celebrity, who was asleep on his bench. He poked his head out from under his blanket of newspapers. "Christ loves every one of you," he shouted. I wrapped my muffler wide across my nose and mouth and stepped in line for my turn at the escalator.

When Michael and I were together we used to buy hot apple croissants at the cart with the awning on the corner.

Michele Orwin

Breakfast at the Umbrella Room, we called it. Then he'd take the step ahead of mine on the escalator, tuck my hands into his coat pockets, and prop me up as we rode one hundred and eighty-eight feet down.

It's the third longest escalator in the Free World, he'd say every day, marveling.

I'd be swallowing hard and closing my eyes. Don't remind me, I'd say, please. If I'd try it just once with my eyes open all the way down, he'd promised to do the cooking for a week.

A bunch of noisy high school kids shoved through the line to race down the left side of the escalator. As my turn came, one boy knocked against me with his bookbag. I grabbed onto the rail to keep my balance, then hesitated. When I looked down I could see myself falling. The stairs rolled by my feet but I couldn't move to catch one.

The crowd gathering behind pushed me forward; the stairs still unfolded too quickly. Then a man to my right touched my elbow; he guided me onto the escalator. "It's all right," he said, close to my ear. "This thing could scare anybody."

"After all," I said, "it is the third longest escalator in the Free World."

At the bottom his hand reappeared to help me off. "There," he said, "we made it."

"Thanks," I called, but he'd blended into the mass of men headed for the subway.

I leaned against the cool stone wall and waited for my heartbeat to slow, my breathing to even out. This wasn't the first time something familiar had slipped its traces and turned terrifying. On and off for months now, I'd suddenly find an ominous quality in ordinary things. I knew if I just took my time, the dizzy feeling would let up.

Captain Video was trolling trashcans early today; he shuffled past me on his morning patrol of the metro station. He stopped, turned around and came back. He stood in front of me and stared.

He carried two copies of *The Washington Post* and a Burger King bag; a bunch of dead yellow mums stuck out of his pocket.

I held my arm over my shoulder bag and hoped he'd go away.

"You okay?" He'd never spoken to me before. Up close he sounded more sane, but he smelled slightly mildewed.

I nodded.

"No, you're not. When white people start looking green, something's wrong. You sick?"

I shook my head.

He inspected me from one side, then the other. "Looks to me like you got a case a hy-po-ven-til-ation. Here." He took a cup of soda out of the Burger King bag and handed me the bag. "You breathe in this and you'll be fine."

There was a curled french fry in the bottom of the bag, brown and greasy. "No, really," I said, "I couldn't."

"Go on, go on. Just put it over your mouth and breathe real slow."

With the bag pressed against my face, I tried not to watch the people stopping to watch me.

"There you go, now you're getting some color."

"You're right," I said, "I do feel better." I gave him back his bag and took a dollar from my wallet. "Could I give you, would you mind?"

"Lots of times I wouldn't take it, you know—" Captain Video picked the french fry from the bottom of the bag and ate it; he stuffed the bill inside his vest—"but I'm saving for a movie. Six dollars they get and it don't even last for two hours." He walked off shaking his head and waving his newspapers. "Craziest damn things," he shouted at someone in a raccoon coat, "going on around here."

She raised the fur collar so it covered her ears.

Roz, the secretary who womanned, as she liked to put it, the front desk at my office, looked up from her mail when I got to work.

"Cold enough for you?" she asked every morning from November through March.

"Isn't it," I answered each day.

"You ought to have a hat. Then you wouldn't lose so much body heat. Lose it from your head and your feet. That's a fact." Roz was our expert on everything.

"Do I look all right?" I still felt a little shaky. There was sweat in the lines of my palms and my tongue tasted like chalk.

"Of course you do. All I'm saying is you need a hat. Maybe you'll get lucky and get one for Christmas." Roz winked.

"That'd be nice," I said, even though I hated hats. But socks, I thought, big thick socks, were something I could use; I'd lost all feeling in eight of my toes.

I pulled off my boots and warmed my feet at the radiator, deliberately delaying a confrontation with my desk. One memo stood out from all the clutter; it looked new and unavoidable.

To: Beth, speech writer, it said. From: Walter, president. Re: Off The Cuff remarks for office X-Mas party. Under Fifteen Minutes. Encourage everyone to Keep Up The Good Work. OMDBE (On My Desk By Eleven).

I ran a sheet of paper through my typewriter; if my concentration held, I could get it done ILTAH (In Less Than An Hour).

I wrote a note on my calendar to remember to call my mother, Naomi, and tell her I couldn't make it this weekend. I'd tell her I'd be up in a week or two. I gnawed a small circle in my lower lip; maybe I ought to go.

The first year after we learned that our mother had cancer, my younger brother, Billy, and I visited our parents one weekend a month. I took the train up from Washington and Billy came in from New York. It was the right thing to do, we told each other. It was, after all, our responsibility to be there, we said. With so little time left and so many loose ends, we had no other choice. But every time we returned to their house, we turned into children again—each month it was harder to make the trip.

The second year, we visited for all the birthdays and holidays, long weekends and half of our vacations. Our older sister, Sharon, and our older brother, Grim, couldn't make it that often. They were too busy with their own lives, they told us. Nothing we do will ever make her happy, Sharon said. Nothing we do will ever make her well, said Grim. Besides, they said, there was no reason for them to come as long as we were there.

But now that Naomi had outlasted the doctors' predictions and was into the third year of living with what had been called an uncommon and incurable type of breast cancer, it was hard to believe she was really all that sick; Billy and I began to find excuses not to go. We stopped believing she was going to die.

I think, I said to Michael, after my last visit with my mother, she's going to be fine.

We were having brunch at the café in the back of the

bookstore where we'd met, where we went every Sunday to read the papers and catch up on each other's news.

He brushed my cheek with the back of his hand. My poor Beth, he said, you really do know that isn't true. Then he went back to reading the business section.

For two years I'd been the one to insist on preparing for the worst with my mother and he'd been the one to persist in hoping for the best. But lately I'd been noticing how his kindness was slipping toward condescension. How often he was distracted and distant. Either his heart and his mind were elsewhere or else he was becoming insensitive. I'd been preparing for that, too.

I do love you, I said, but I think it's time for me to move out. I didn't know I thought that until I said it. I wasn't sure what he could say that would make me back down.

He put his newspaper on the table. You're serious? he asked; we usually tried so hard not to be.

I've got this terrible feeling, I said, you won't even notice I'm not there.

Then I guess you'll never understand, he said. And I'm worn out from trying. I don't think I can try anymore.

Look, if there's someone else, I said, surprised he was angry when I was the one who felt hurt, I'm not really sure I want you to tell me.

I am not, he said later, as he watched me pack the photographs and all the pieces of scrimshaw we'd collected in our four years together, the only one who's insensitive. I really do wish, he said, this didn't have to happen.

I hadn't spoken to him in six months. Though my friends and family told me otherwise, I knew it was the right decision.

. . .

The intercom light blinked. "It's eleven," Walt said, "and I don't see my speech on my desk."

"Give me fifteen more minutes."

"You got it."

I produced the speech, but when Walt stood up to address the troops, as he called his staff, the party had been going on for an hour. What Walt had to say didn't matter as much as the fact that we were running out of white wine, and the cheese they'd bought was overripe. Walt addressed the troops assembled in the conference room while Roz took up a collection for another gallon jug of Mountain Chablis. Greg insisted on going with her to return the cheese and demand another half pound of Jarlsberg.

"You look tired." Walt poured the last of the wine in his coffee mug. "Why don't you go home?"

"Took the words right out of my mouth," I said. I'd been writing his speeches for five years; it was our oldest joke.

"Before you leave," he said, "I want to see you in my office."

At the first Christmas party he'd said that to me, I was sure he was going to tell me I was fired. At the second party, I was hopeful he would offer me a raise. By now I knew to expect some small, carefully chosen gift.

I followed him down the hall. It was hard not to imitate his lopsided gait. His back was bad and getting worse; he walked with his shoulders tipped forward, his right hip at an angle. For years Roz had insisted the Alexander technique could have him straightened out in no time. For years he'd argued nothing could cure a degenerating disc and old age. His granddaughter was in her first year of college; he was entitled to look his age.

Walt unlocked his desk and took out a flat gold box tied with a red bow.

"I got you something." He tilted back in his large leather chair and smiled.

I didn't want to open it. I'd been unable to face the stores this year; I didn't have presents for anyone.

"Open it," he said, "so I can see how you like it."

Underneath all the layers of folded tissue paper was a white angora beret. Roz must have told him about all the body heat I was losing.

I hugged Walt so quickly he didn't have time to object. "Thank you," I said, "it's just what I needed. I don't have one."

"I know," he said, proud of himself. "Try it on, it'll look nice against your dark hair."

"Next week," I promised. If I didn't leave right away, I'd start to cry and Walt wouldn't know what to do with me.

It was too early to go home; I was afraid I might run into Drew Morrison, and I still hadn't been able to face him since the one night last month when I'd mistaken loneliness for interest and stayed over at his place. In the morning he'd used the word "relationship" and I didn't know how to tell him I didn't want one.

I walked slowly in spite of the cold. I invented errands to delay going home. I bought daisies to replace the ones that were wilting in my front hall. I tried to retrieve the skirt I'd left at the cleaner's three weeks ago, but the sign said they'd be closed through New Year's. All I had left on my list was a turkey sandwich for dinner. I stopped at Gleason's Market, where Joe, the owner, was always the last one to put up his Christmas decorations. Today Santa's face smiled in the window above spray-painted snow; it would be smiling there till February.

"Don't tell me," Joe said, "you're alone again this weekend."

Since I'd stopped seeing Michael, my slow social life was open to public discussion. More than once Joe'd mixed up my order trying to introduce me to the man who had corned beef on rye every Friday. He'd even offered the name of his nephew, a middle-aged single father living in Seattle.

"I like it this way," I said.

"That's what you say." He threw in the lettuce and tomato for free; he gave me an extra pickle spear. "For the holidays," he said, "I can afford to be a sport."

A man at the corner had rows of red poinsettias in the back of a white van; little packages of mistletoe wrapped in plastic were displayed on the door. "Do your Christmas shopping late," he said. "Bring a plant home for a friend."

I shook my head. The wind was making my eyes tear and my nose run. My muffler was getting wet and irritating my face. I could feel a rash starting on my chin.

"Maybe you want a watch for your boyfriend? A silk tie? A real cashmere scarf?" He slid open the side door of the van. "Good quality," he said, "good prices."

I kept walking; but even with my head down to block the wind, I spotted the back of Drew's Burberry coat going into our building a few steps ahead of me. It was too cold to keep on dodging him; I wanted to go home. When he stopped at his mailbox, he saw me coming and waited.

"I was on my way up to give you this." He held a bottle of Irish Cream Liqueur in a box with four small glasses, on sale at the liquor store down the block for $10.95. "Just friends again." He offered his hand.

"Good friends," I told him. "Come by this weekend for a drink."

"Since you put it that way—" he propped his attaché

case against the elevator door to keep it from closing on us and leaned toward me—"I'm still free New Year's Eve."

"I wish I could," I lied, "but I'm busy."

"You know where to reach me." He got off on the floor below mine taking the Irish Cream with him.

My one-bedroom apartment was in a plain white brick building just off Dupont Circle. Its only charm was the way my bedroom filled with early-morning light. It had been the perfect size for me when I took it after Jim and I separated, and I'd held on to it even while I lived with Michael, for the extra income from the sublet, I'd told him. For the feeling of knowing it's there if I ever need it, I said. But now, after ten years, it was starting to seem crowded, a little dismal. The walls needed paint, the floors had to be sanded.

I threw out the old flowers and put the new ones in their place. I took off my boots and ate my sandwich standing up in front of the television while I caught the end of the news. Then I called Billy.

Every Friday night we checked in with each other. Billy and I were each looking for something, but in all our Friday night talks we'd yet to figure out what it was. Billy had switched cities, changed jobs, run through roommates and hadn't come across it, while I'd stayed in one place to search for years, and still it eluded me.

Now, if we weren't visiting our parents for the weekend, we needed reassurance it was all right. If we were living alone, we needed company. Billy lived part time with Cheryl; it was his longest and most serious romance since he'd fallen in love with his piano teacher when he was thirteen, but he was resolutely committed to no commitment. For himself. For me, he wanted something more permanent. He was always trying to talk me into getting back with Michael. Billy'd been the one to find Michael for me; he couldn't forgive me for losing him.

Four years ago Billy moved in with me while he was trying to decide where he'd live next. Every night that summer we spent hours trying to get a handle on his future while we sat at one of the sidewalk tables in the bookstore café near my apartment. The tables were placed so close to each other, we usually ended up talking to the people on either side; Billy was always less shy with strangers than he was with people who knew him well. One warm July night, Billy was halfway into his brownie with ice cream and hot fudge when the waiter brought a slice of carrot cake to the man sitting next to us.

Excuse me, Billy said, but if God wanted us to have carrots for dessert, He wouldn't have invented chocolate. I lowered my head; the man laughed. Chicago, Billy said, or some place in the Midwest. That's the only area where they teach you to laugh like that.

Chicago, the man said. My name's Michael, he said, then he looked over at me. If Billy hadn't been watching me so closely, I might have thought of something to say. The man was clearly good-looking; he had nice eyes, a great laugh, no wedding ring. But all I could do was smile and nod. I let Billy do the talking, never expecting he'd ask this Michael person over for dinner the next night.

Then it's set, Billy said. Tomorrow. He gave him my address.

I turned in my seat and stepped on Billy's foot. Sorry, I said, these tables are so small.

Fine, Michael said to Billy. I'm looking forward to it, he said to me.

If you'd like to bring someone, I said.
No, he said, I live alone.

It's one thing, I said to Billy, when you bring someone you don't know back to your place. It's something else when you ask someone over to mine. I only have two chairs.
We'll sit on the floor, Billy said.
What if he wears a suit?
He won't, Billy said. Trust me.
But Michael did wear a suit and spent the first five minutes apologizing that he didn't have time to go home after work to change. Billy told Michael to have a seat, make himself comfortable. Then he left us together, while he ran out to pick up a pizza. An hour later he called to say he'd run into a couple of new friends and wouldn't be back; he was having the pizza delivered. Some day you'll thank me, he said. You're perfect for each other.
He'd left me no choice, I had to be friendly. When Michael was still there for breakfast, Billy went to Conran's and bought another chair.
You'd probably have more room, Billy said after a month, if you'd live at his apartment.
It's too soon, I said. I've got this feeling there's still someone in the background. I found a blue eyeliner pencil in his medicine cabinet and a cream silk scarf in his closet. She must have been blond, I said. He's probably going to go back to her.
If he is, Billy said, he's got a funny way of doing it.
By the time Billy decided he'd head for New York, I was spending six days out of seven at Michael's. I'd already moved my winter clothes over to his apartment when we went to his law firm's Christmas party; I'd even filled out a change of address for my *Newsweek* subscription. And then

I met Cynthia, the youngest associate in the firm. A tall, thin blonde in a pink suede skirt and white satin blouse. All cheekbones and hipbones, she was wearing diamond earrings that I overheard her tell one of the partners she'd bought for herself with her Christmas bonus.

She's lovely to look at, I said to Michael at that first law firm party, biting hard on the swizzle stick in my third drink.

Whatever Michael said, his arm around me the whole time, it wasn't what I wanted to hear.

You make a handsome couple, I said.

Cynthia watched Michael, I watched Cynthia. The pain in my chest wouldn't go away, so I kept talking. She's probably very intelligent, I said. She looks like she's very successful for someone so young.

Michael took my hand in both of his. When you're done, he said, let's go someplace where we can both have fun.

I promised I'd never mention her again. Though I did comment once how sorry I was when I heard she didn't make partner and had to leave the firm. I didn't ask where she went, but I was always afraid it wasn't far enough away.

"A funny thing's happening," I told Billy when I called him after I'd finished my turkey sandwich. "I'm starting to get lonely. I think it's beginning to show. Sometimes I feel like I'm that sad little puppy in the book we used to read, wandering around begging people to pat me on the head and hold me in their lap. Do you ever have that feeling?"

"Story of my life," he said. "Who knows, maybe someone will give us a home." His "call-waiting" line clicked. "I better take that," he said. "I'll get back to you in a couple minutes."

When my phone rang again I was sure it was Billy. I picked up the receiver, expecting to continue our conversation. "First," I said, "there was this guy on the subway . . ."

"We're at the hospital." It took me a minute to register my father's voice. "No one knows for certain what's going on, but they say it might be tonight."

"What are you talking about?"

"What the hell's the matter with you, Beth? Your mother is dying and I want you here as soon as possible."

"That's ridiculous," I said, "I just spoke to her." He'd already hung up.

I tore off a paper towel and scrubbed the spots from my refrigerator. I'd spoken to Naomi yesterday, she hadn't sounded any different. With my fingernail, I worked out the rubbery strip of dirt caked between the rim of the sink and the Formica counter top. I was planning to call her tonight and tell her I'd be up next week. If she'd asked, I probably would have made it this weekend. I polished the chrome-plated surface of my toaster oven. I emptied the crumbs from the bottom shelf. Michael used to say he always knew when I was upset—it was the only time I cleaned the kitchen. I worked so hard cleaning the wall behind the stove, I took the paint off. For over two years, I'd rehearsed that one phone call so many times in my mind, it was hard to believe this time it was real.

I was scraping the grease off the oven with a single-edge razor when the doorbell rang.

"About that drink," Drew said. He'd changed into starched jeans and a red plaid flannel shirt. He was carrying a bottle of sherry in a cloth sack.

"It's not a good time for me," I said. "I've just had some bad news."

He kicked the door closed behind him. "Then you shouldn't be alone."

Before I could argue with him, the phone rang and I left Drew standing by the door.

"Where'd you go?" Roz said. "The party was just getting started and you disappeared." I could hear restaurant noise in the background. "We're at the Timberlakes' around the corner. Come meet us," she said.

"I can't," I said. Drew made himself comfortable on my sofa; he put his feet up on my coffee table. "I just got a call from my father, he thinks my mother is . . ."

"Now listen to me, Beth," Roz said, her voice suddenly sober. "It might be a false alarm. I know what I'm talking about. Sometimes people look like they're taking a turn for the worse and then they go right into remission. It happens all the time. Do you want me to come over?"

Drew was reading the TV schedule. "No," I said. "I'll be fine."

"Take care of yourself," Roz said. "And let me know what happens."

"I'm glad you told them no," Drew said. "I didn't feel like going out either."

He took the sherry out of its sack and put it on the table. His apartment was the mirror of mine; he walked around my kitchen as if he lived there. "Where do you keep your small glasses?"

"I don't have any," I said. "And I don't . . ." The phone interrupted me.

"Have you heard?" It was Billy.

"Yes," I said. "Maybe it's just a false alarm?"

"In a way," he said, "I hope it isn't. God, what an awful thing to say."

"No," I said. "I kind of feel the same way. It's gone on for such a long time."

Drew was searching through my records. "Something

light?" he asked. I was trying to listen to Billy. I nodded at Drew.

"Jesus," Billy said, "how did we piss away all that time?"

"I don't know," I said. "Maybe there wasn't so much after all."

"Maybe—" his voice started to trail off. "If you need me, I'll be here."

"I know," I said. "I'm here for you, too."

"Another guy?" Drew said.

"My brother. Look, what I've been trying to tell you is that my mother's dying."

He'd poured the sherry into beer glasses Michael and I had won at the beach. He handed me one. "It's a good thing I'm here," he said. "I'll take care of you. Sit down, relax."

"I can't." I knew there were a hundred things I should be doing and at the same time I knew there was nothing I could do.

Drew looked through my refrigerator, found some shriveled-up celery and a container of yogurt. "This is it? We really ought to go to my place so I can fix us a nice dinner. A caesar salad, mushroom omelets."

I closed the refrigerator; he'd gotten fingerprints on the handle. I'd have to clean it again as soon as he left.

"Some other time," I said. "Not tonight."

He swirled the sherry around in his glass, then looked up at me. "There is another guy."

"Drew, can't you understand? I just want to be alone."

"Now?" he said. "It's only nine o'clock."

I started to pack my clothes, then I remembered I'd better water my plants, but I stopped halfway through that and returned to my closet, then back to the plants. When the phone rang, I jumped and dropped the watering can; water spilled all over the floor.

"Listen, Beth," Sharon said, "I want you to pick up the car and meet me at the airport. I'll be in around one."

Sharon, older by six years, never spoke, she only lectured, she commanded and directed, she made decisions, definite and irrevocable. She was an attorney long before, she always said, women made it their pet profession. All it took to keep her life running smoothly was for everyone else to follow her orders. She went from home to office with a trail of secretaries and maids to keep her on schedule, take care of details. I fit in somewhere in a series of subordinates.

"I can't pick you up," I said.

"What do you mean you can't? Of course you can. I want you to pick up Hersh's car and meet me at Newark Airport."

"Take a cab," I said. "That's what I usually do."

"Thanks, kiddo. Then do me a favor and tell Hersh I'll try to be there by early afternoon, if I can. What a mess. Her timing is perfect."

"I'll tell him," I said. I'd been pacing and I ended up by my dresser with the phone cord coiled around me. I had to walk in circles to get back to the bed.

"And, Bethie, please, bring something nice to wear to the, you know. Not one of those Indian things."

I never meant to obey her, but somehow I usually did. I took the brown batik dress from my suitcase and replaced it with my black suit. I'd need shoes. And stockings. Don't you have a dark bag? It was Naomi's voice. What are you going to wear over it? You can't possibly wear that navy down coat, it's old and too short. Naomi again. What difference does it make? I argued with her the way I always did. You won't even be there, I said for the first time.

I slammed the suitcase shut and forced the lock so it jammed. I had to pry it open with a screwdriver and lock it one more time.

I was getting ready for bed when the phone rang again.

"Wake you?" Grim asked.

"Not yet," I said. "I feel like I've been sleepwalking all night."

Grim used to walk in his sleep. He'd leave his room and wander around the house, in the morning we'd find him curled up by the hot-water heater in the basement. Sharon ground her teeth; she wore her molars down until she had to sleep with a guard in her mouth. And Billy had his blanket with the satin strip, then later just the strip, after the blanket was turned into rags. All I needed was a night light. Our parents tried a different cure for each of us; none of them took. Naomi claimed Grim still sleepwalked through his life. How else, she always asked, could he have thrown away so much promise?

"I need your help," Grim said. "You'll have to cover for me awhile. I can't make it till after Christmas. I was supposed to take all the kids this weekend—getting out of it's a bear." Grim had been married twice before Lonnie; for Christmas and summer vacations, they took his three children.

Oldest of all of us, Grim's life was full of magic and mystery. He'd start a family, then disappear, show up again to juggle ex-wives and children. Even with his record of wrecked families, Lonnie was willing to add to his collection of kids. She'd been trying to get pregnant for a year. Grim was willing to devote his sabbatical to her effort.

"How can you wait?" I said. "From the way Hersh sounded, it might be tonight."

"He's overreacting. She's too tough to give up so fast. Besides, if anything happens, you can call."

"But he just did," I said.

"Well, whatever," Grim said, "I've got no other choice."

Grim used to say he never made choices, life always screwed them up anyway. I'll just do what comes next, he'd say, and he usually did.

I was beyond feeling tired, but well past being able to stay awake. I changed into the old T-shirt of Michael's I still wore to bed and flipped on the bathroom light I left burning each night. As I brushed my teeth I turned away from the mirror. Lately I'd been seeing traces of my mother's face in my own. The resemblance was a trick, the connection between us had always been so vague. My face was rounder, her nose thinner, our eyes different shades. Our lives on tracks so distant from each other it always seemed impossible we were actually related. I rinsed out the sink, carefully scrubbing the soap off the faucets in order to keep my hands from searching for, and finding, the way hers had, a large, awful lump.

2

The cab arrived at 6:15; a cone of sandalwood incense burned on the dash, a silver-winged scarab hung from the mirror. "Show you White House," the driver said. "Everyone wants to see White House."

"No, that's all right," I said. The music on the radio was so loud, I was sure he couldn't hear me. "Just the train station."

"White House first," he insisted, "then I know how to find train station."

"One way to Newark," I told the man behind the ticket counter.

"Can't do that." He smiled.

"Look," I said. I was ready for a fight.

He smiled again. "Can't let a good-looking woman leave town and never come back. Besides, round trip is cheaper."

"Fine," I said, "round trip is fine. But please, hurry."

"No hurry," he said. "The train doesn't leave for forty-five minutes."

I took a window seat out of habit; I no longer watched the scenery—a long stretch of abandoned factories and run-down motels, a few iridescent green ponds, the Philadelphia Zoo, the sign saying "Trenton Makes, The World Takes," and the suburban neighborhood in southern New Jersey where every house had an above-ground pool in the backyard.

I'd made this trip so often since Naomi became sick, it had become a strange break in my life. There were times when I'd feel a funny kind of freedom. And then I'd feel guilty; it wasn't the idea of my mother's death that brought on this sensation, I'd tell myself. It had to come from the feeling of being suspended between the family I'd left long ago in New Jersey and the people who filled up my life in Washington. I was temporarily out of reach of all of them. But this time I felt only a queasiness so deep, I didn't dare even drink a cup of coffee. I had my bags in the aisle before the conductor called out, "Newark, next stop. Next stop, Newark."

When my grandparents lived in Newark, I used to think their house was very far away, in another country; we hardly ever saw them. Naomi would only agree to dinner at their house every Passover and four Sunday visits in between. Twice a year Hersh invited his parents to our house.

She's embarrassed by them, Sharon explained to Billy and me as we sat on the floor in her bedroom. Mother is embarrassed because Grandma and Grandpa are old and poor and they're from Russia. If her parents were still alive, she wouldn't want to see them either.

Our mother never talked about her parents. As far as Billy and I knew, she never had any. We had one set of grandparents, one set of parents, and Mary.

But they're my family, Hersh said.

Exactly, Naomi said. Your family, not mine. They've always made that perfectly clear.

You're the one, Hersh began.

Who took you away, Naomi finished for him. Someone ought to tell them you really never left.

We're going today, we overheard Hersh tell Naomi one Sunday morning, that's all there is to it.

Naomi didn't answer him. She walked into the playroom where Billy and I pretended we weren't listening to their argument.

Dress nicely, children, she said. We have to visit your grandparents. Then she went into our rooms and picked out the clothes she wanted us to wear.

Sharon and Grim were busy with their friends that day. And friends, Naomi believed, were more important than family. Your family will grow up and leave you, she'd say, but with friends the worst that happens is they have other plans. Naomi would have met The Girls for lunch if Hersh hadn't made such a commotion about visiting his family.

I don't ask much, he always said when he asked for something. It's only one day.

Billy brought along his frogmen and I took two of the Ginny dolls I was forced to collect but always hated. We put the armrest down between us in the backseat of the car. The floor became the treacherous waters of Battle Creek, home of the fearless frogmen. My half of the seat was the quiet countryside where the unsuspecting Ginnys went to picnic. They had a lovely straw basket and little straw hats. Naomi had bought them tiny patent-leather shoes and purses to match the ones she'd bought for me. Prim and dainty, they sat on my white handkerchief nibbling imaginary cream-cheese sandwiches, when suddenly, out of nowhere, the frogmen attacked and dragged the Ginnys kicking and screaming over the hill of the armrest and threw them into Battle Creek where they drowned. We cheered and clapped and poked them with our feet to make sure they were dead.

Can't you children play quietly? Naomi asked. She lowered the visor on her side of the windshield and looked back at us in the mirror. We nodded.

Count cars, Hersh said. Beth, you take blue, Bill, you take red.

One, two, three. Billy started before me.

That's not red, that's maroon, I said. You cheated.

To yourselves, Hersh ordered, count to yourselves. Don't tell us till we get there.

Billy opened the window a crack so he wouldn't get carsick and Naomi told him to close it; she fixed her hair.

Billy had copped four Tootsie Rolls from Naomi's company candy dish; he coughed while he took off the wrappers and passed me one. If we made any noise, Naomi would catch us, so I tucked mine inside my cheek and Billy let his dissolve in the middle of his tongue.

Just before we got to our grandparents' house, Naomi put down the visor and inspected us again. William, how did your face get dirty? Beth, why is it you always manage to look like an unmade bed?

Hersh parked the car, then turned to look at us: Well?

We're sorry, I said.

For what?

I don't know, but we didn't mean it.

What the hell's the matter with you, are you some kind of idiot? I'm asking how many cars. Bill?

Seventeen, he said. I knew he was making it up.

Fourteen, I reported. Sometimes I liked to let Billy win.

Aunt Rose and Aunt Sylvia were at the car before we could get out. Uncle Sidney and Uncle Leo waited on the path to the house. Aunt Essie, Aunt Bertha, cousin Seymour, cousin Milton crowded together on the porch. Our grandmother waved to us from behind the screen door. Naomi sighed and waved back.

The twin Pekingese started yapping when Aunt Rose opened the door. They circled my feet and nipped at my ankles.

You want to pet Minsky? Aunt Sylvia held up a dog; with the side of her foot she kept the other one quiet.

I looked to Naomi for permission. Naomi didn't like animals because they were dirty. What she objected to most, she said, was the way Hersh's family let their dogs in the dining room. She was sure their dogs slept in the kitchen. One Passover we had to leave early because she found a hair in her gefilte fish.

Our grandfather sat in his chair in the front room where our cousin Milton kept his tropical fish. Our grandfather sat in that room, read the paper, drank his glass of tea, and listened to the radio. When he was tired, he slept on the daybed.

He was tall, but we always saw him sitting down, always wearing a dark suit. He had dark eyes and a scratchy black beard and a large black spot high on his cheek where more hair grew. He looked like the giant in "Jack and the Beanstalk."

Pop—Hersh touched him on the shoulder so the old man would look up from his paper. He kissed him on the head. How are you?

After nearly fifty years in this country, our grandfather couldn't speak more than a few words of English. He answered in Yiddish; Aunt Rose translated.

He's telling your father he's not so good. He doesn't sleep well. All night, he says, with the bubbles from the fish tank. All night with the bubbles, how can he sleep?

So move, Aunt Rose said in English, then Yiddish. She raised her arms in the air to show she was ready to throw him out of the house herself. So get yourself another room if you're not happy.

Our grandfather held out his hands to us. Come, he said. I wanted Billy to go first, Billy waited for me. I got to kiss the side of his face that didn't have the big black spot.

Tea. Coffee. Come, Aunt Essie said. She led us into the dining room to see their green parakeet, Petie, perched in his cage in one corner of the room.

Sit, sit, Aunt Bertha said. Naomi looked over at Petie and took a chair on the opposite side of the table.

Aunt Sylvia served Hersh a glass of cold borscht. She put a bowl of steaming boiled potatoes next to his plate. Aunt Rose poured Cott Concord grape soda into the green glasses in front of Billy and me. Wait till you see what I got for you, she said. Your Uncle Sidney just brought them back from the bakery.

Aunt Essie came in carrying two charlotte russes.

We looked over at Naomi.

Go ahead, go ahead, Aunt Rose said, enjoy. I've never seen such scaredy-cats in my life.

I don't know what's gotten into them, Hersh apologized for us. They've been acting badly all day.

Children don't take after neighbors, you know, Aunt Essie said. She smiled at Naomi.

Never mind, Aunt Rose said, just look at that face. She leaned over to cup my chin in her hand. She'll be a beauty some day, as soon as she loses the baby fat. If you ask me, she's the spitting image of Essie.

Aunt Essie was short, with curly hair and bad eyes. She smelled of cooked cabbage. From the way Naomi watched me, I knew I'd better outgrow looking like Essie along with the baby fat.

And the little one, Aunt Sylvia said. She combed Billy's hair with her fingers. He'll be the brains in the family, wait and see. An Einstein, she decided.

What are you talking about? Aunt Rose demanded. You've never heard him play the piano? He's a Van Cliburn if there ever was one.

Naomi didn't say a word. Hersh just kept on eating. His sisters filled his plate with herring in sour cream, with stuffed cabbage, with warm fruit compote.

Billy and I finished quickly so we could leave the table, but as soon as we were done, Aunt Bertha brought us fruit slices coated in sugar, cookies with circles of raspberry jam, pieces of halvah, and chocolate-covered marshmallow twists.

Really, Bert, Naomi said, they've had enough.

Aunt Bertha sat down as if she'd been shot. Bertha looked over at Hersh. Hersh kept on eating.

You may be excused, Naomi said.

Our little grandmother said something. She wants you to sit on her lap, Aunt Rose told us.

This time I made Billy go first. We took turns on her lap while she held us by the ears and kissed us right in the middle of the forehead the way she kissed our father. We knew when she said something in Yiddish, rapped her knuckles on the table, and everyone else knocked on wood too, she was through with us.

Go, Aunt Sylvia said. And we ran out of the room.

We headed for the front of the house, then remembered our grandfather sitting in his chair like the giant at the top of the beanstalk. Billy pulled me in the other direction, out the back door and up the stairs.

Cousin Milton, Uncle Leo, and some men we didn't know sat around a card table playing pinochle.

Hey, Shirley Temple—Uncle Leo took the cigar out of his mouth—come here. I want to show you something. Bet you didn't know your Uncle Leo was a magician.

He snapped his fingers by my ear and produced a dime. He slipped his other hand under my dress and pinched my behind.

And you, Arthur Rubinstein, you want to see what I can find in your ears besides wax? He snapped near Billy's ear and turned up a quarter. See? And you thought your father was the only one who knew how to make any money around here. Enough, he said and lit his cigar. Now go play outside.

Billy flipped his baseball cards on the sidewalk. I sat on the porch steps and pressed my Silly Putty against the color comic strips in the newspaper. I had to go to the bathroom, but I was afraid to go back inside. I crossed and recrossed my legs until I couldn't wait any longer. Come with me, Billy, please.

He refused.

I offered him my dime, the other Tootsie Roll, the cardboard crown from the charlotte russe, and he still refused. I said he could come in and watch and he gave in.

We sneaked back into the house just as Naomi was kissing everyone goodbye. Now what? she said.

I didn't want to tell her. There was something about our having to go to the bathroom that usually got her annoyed.

No more food, she said. Please wait in the car.

We ran out the door.

Just a minute, Hersh said. I want you to go back and say goodbye properly. He marched us back in.

We let ourselves be kissed by our aunts; we let our uncles

pat our heads. Our grandfather was asleep so we didn't have to face him again. Then we started out the door one more time.

Your grandmother, Hersh said, I want you to go back and kiss your grandmother goodbye. You may not be seeing her for a very long time.

I stood on my toes to kiss my grandmother's soft white cheek; I touched her face.

Softer than a baby's bottom, Hersh said. Your grandmother has the softest skin in the world. He always talked about her soft skin and her eyes as green as the sea.

Finally we got back in the car, put down the armrest, and took out our toys.

There, Naomi said when she'd settled herself in the front seat. I hope you children remembered to use the bathroom before we left.

One night, a few weeks later, Hersh didn't come home until just as I was getting into bed. I heard him open the door and I ran down the stairs to see him; whenever he was away, he always brought us something.

Hersh stood in the front hall with his hat still on his head and his coat in his arms. I'd never seen him cry before.

Your grandmother is dead, he said. May she rest in peace.

I put my hands on his ears and kissed him in the middle of his forehead the way she used to; he smiled a little, then sent me back to bed.

In the morning, we sat on the floor in Sharon's room while she explained to us how Jewish people have to be buried right away. Almost as soon as they close their eyes, she said.

Billy and I stayed home from school, but we couldn't go to the funeral. We spent the day with Mary, once our nurse, now our special friend, and asked God to be nice to our grandmother. We ate all the Swiss chocolates and the purple grapes out of the basket someone sent. Then Sharon came home from the cemetery and told us we were supposed to tear our clothes. She got a pair of scissors and cut up my red dress.

What are you afraid of most? I said to Billy after Mary had put us to bed.

The rule was, we had to say our first thought. The rule was, we couldn't lie.

That some day Mary will die too.

She won't, I said. That doesn't count.

Okay, he said. I'm afraid our parents will die and we'll be orphans.

If they ever do that, I said, I'll run away.

Hersh came upstairs to change his clothes. He looked in on us, then switched off the night light in the hall.

Last year, when Michael's grandmother died, his parents waited five days to tell him. She'd passed away in the morning and was buried that same afternoon. She was an old woman, they said, she'd been sick a long time. They thought he'd be too busy to get to Chicago in time for the funeral. They were worried he'd be upset by the news.

I was less surprised at what they did than he was. The one time I'd met Michael's parents, it was clear they treated their only son with a reverence more appropriate for the Pope. It was true he was the first in his family to go to college, then to law school, but I was less impressed by it than they were. And because of that, they were less impressed with me.

Michael sat in his chair brooding all night. I'm a grown man, he said, I had a right to know.

Come to bed, I said, it's getting late. I rubbed the place in the back of his neck where I knew it knotted up when he was upset.

If I could remember what she looked like, he said, I wouldn't feel so bad.

I know, I said, I tried to do the same thing. But all I could think about was my father telling me to kiss my grandmother because I wasn't going to see her for a very long time. I never figured out how he knew.

I didn't tell him, but I always thought he knew that after her death I became more careful about saying goodbye. Even those weekend mornings when Michael would sleep in and I'd only be going down the block to pick up breakfast, I'd tiptoe into the bedroom and lightly kiss his forehead before leaving the apartment. I'll be back, I'd whisper. Sometimes he'd roll over in bed and smile.

3

The hospital looked too familiar. I'd been there a few weeks before when Naomi had an operation to have a catheter inserted in her chest. It was a new procedure being tried on patients whose veins had collapsed. The only side effect, we learned afterward, was that Naomi would be bedridden for the rest of her life; at the time, her doctors said she could go on living for a year or more.

I walked through the turnstile and waited while the tight-lipped woman behind the reception desk filled out a special pass. She made it clear she'd do it though she didn't like it one bit.

"And where do you think you're going?" she said to the man who came in after me.

"My wife," he said, "they brought her in last night."

"Well, you can't see her now," she said. "You come back when it's time. Schedule's posted right on the wall."

It wasn't regular visiting hours. I didn't even know when they were. Our family had permission to visit any time. One nurse told me the hospital extended this courtesy to relatives of all patients who were terminally ill. Hersh and Naomi thought the special treatment was only natural for people of their standing in the community.

To them the hospital was more like a hotel they'd booked through a bad travel agent; it lacked bellhops and room service and an attentive concierge. The service was poor, the staff hostile. Still, they expected extra towels and the room made up during breakfast. If you know how to ask, Naomi used to instruct all of us, it's not hard to get what you want. She still believed if she could just be charming and gracious enough the doctors would be won over and she'd be sent home with a clean bill of health.

Because Naomi had been in and out of the hospital so often during the past two years, she and Hersh had been forced to do much of their entertaining in her private room on the fourth floor.

Their friends dropped in bringing sandwiches and cookies, packets of instant coffee with and without caffeine, powdered creamer and artificial sweetener. They sent fruit baskets and candy boxes, flowers to fill every ledge, bottles of perfume, and dozens of cards to tack on top of other cards on the corkboard on the wall. Fat best-sellers had to be stacked in the corner on piles of newspapers and magazines. A few of The Girls brought fancy shower caps and scarves for Naomi to wear so they wouldn't have to see how much hair she'd lost. And the private-duty nurses Hersh hired were told to swipe chairs from other rooms, to lift a few more towels to keep on hand.

Waiting for Next Week

When the first of their friends came in the morning, Naomi or Hersh or one of the nurses would call down to the front desk for hot water and soon there'd be instant coffee and Danish butter cookies for everyone.

Lunchtime friends brought sandwiches from the deli, whole-milk mozzarella cheese and Genoa salami from the Italian market, pâté and Brie from the specialty shops.

Hersh and Naomi never traveled without a bottle of scotch and a bottle of vodka in a black leather case. Naomi, always the good hostess, brought the black leather case along to the hospital. Their friends who came late in the afternoon showed up with mixers and glasses, jars of olives and nuts, crackers and cheese spreads. And Naomi would sit in her satin bed jacket making sure everyone was eating and drinking, telling Hersh who needed a refill, which one needed him to fix another cracker.

But her friends had migrated to Florida for the season between Thanksgiving and Passover; only a few would be by to visit this time. Besides, Naomi had stopped eating three days ago.

Some joke, she'd said on the phone. All my life I've tried to diet. Now, when it doesn't matter anymore, I'm losing weight.

It matters, I said. You've got to eat.

I can't. I've lost all interest in food.

When they go off food, Roz said, it's usually a bad sign. Then again, it might be nothing.

I walked down the fourth-floor hall to the nurses' station where red and green crepe paper looped from the ceiling, a "Happy Holidays" banner hung from the desk. There was a Norfolk pine in a red pot with a gold star on the top. A Styrofoam snowman sat in a drift of cotton balls; he wore a black hat, a hypodermic needle was stuck in his side.

Hersh stood in the corridor resting his head against the wall. I'd seen him do that to keep himself from crying. He'd rest his forehead against something cool, or else he'd drink water very quickly to loosen the lump in his throat.

His hair, still thick at seventy-two, curled over the back of his collar. Since Naomi had been confined to bed, he'd stopped going for his weekly haircuts. And he'd stopped wearing his three-piece suits; instead he wore old V-neck cardigans with holes at the elbows. His shoulders had started to turn inward and he'd put on weight that settled in a slight bulge above his belt. The age spots must have appeared on his hands a long time ago, but each time I saw them they surprised me.

Hersh had been talking about retiring for years, but he was sure if he stopped working he'd waste away and die. Naomi thought it was working that would kill him. Neither of them ever considered that she'd be the first to go. Wives were supposed to outlive their husbands, and Naomi was one woman who always did exactly what she was supposed to do. Her getting sick was so completely out of character, they still thought it had to be a mistake. Hersh bargained with the doctors from the day they made the diagnosis. I'll give up the business, I'll retire, he told them. We'll move to Florida, she'll be fine. But the doctors said moving was out of the question once she started her treatments. Naomi herself said she was too tired to move. If you'd done it sooner, she said, who knows if this would have happened. The doctors said it would have, Hersh knew it wouldn't. It's my fault, he said. For once she didn't argue with him.

I touched Hersh's back. "How is she?"

"It's incredible. Yesterday they thought she wouldn't last the night. Today she's sitting up in bed talking."

"What?" I said. You mean you called me here for nothing? I caught myself wanting to ask.

"Now don't get your hopes up, they still say it won't be more than a week. But you ought to see her. She looks terrific. Go on in, you won't believe it."

Naomi sat up in bed, wearing her mauve satin bed jacket over her hospital gown. Tubes ran from her nose and mouth. More tubes sprouted out from under the sheets and fed into plastic bags on both sides of the bed. There was a metal stand on one side where the containers of glucose hung and dripped fluid into the catheter in her chest. Her arms and legs were swollen and bruised. Her stomach was distended; with the pillow she kept over it, she looked pregnant. She had scabs on her face and hands from the shingles. Her hair had fallen out once, grown in completely, then fallen out again. There was the same covering of gray fuzz now that she'd had a year ago. And her face had narrowed, making her large dark eyes so enormous I was sure I could see all of Naomi in them. Today in her eyes I saw fear.

"Darling," Naomi said and tried to hold out her hands; the nails she'd kept long and well-cared for were short and colorless, rippled and brittle. "Still don't have a decent coat, I see."

"You wouldn't recognize me any other way." I ran my hand over the fuzz on her head. I kissed her scabbed cheeks and held her hands full of black-and-blue marks. I took a deep breath and waited for the numbness to set in; it always did. The shock that I felt the first time I saw her in a wheelchair, a woman half the size of my mother and nearly hairless, had lessened over time. She'd fought so hard to act as if her appearance hadn't changed, I had learned to ignore the changes. "Have you started eating again?"

"I can't," Naomi said. "Just the thought of food makes me tired."

"I can smell them bringing the trays around. I bet I could snag you one if you want."

"And where would I put it?" she said.

Hersh came into the room. "Doesn't she look terrific?"

"If I'm so beautiful," Naomi said, "why won't they let me have a mirror?"

"Don't talk," Hersh told her. "With those tubes in her mouth she shouldn't talk too much."

"What else have I got to do?" she said.

"Can I get you some ice to wet your lips? Do you want me to call the nurse?" he asked her.

"Just sit down, would you please?"

For months now, the nicer Hersh got, the meaner Naomi was to him. Sometimes I wish he'd leave me alone, she'd stage whisper.

But he wouldn't. He was with her every minute she was awake. He helped her walk to the bathroom when she could still get out of bed, and when she was bedridden he overcame his squeamishness and brought her the bedpan. Though he'd never cooked before and swore he never would again, he learned to make toast and tea and served it to her even when she insisted she wasn't hungry. He watched the nurses change the dressings and learned how to do it, just in case she ever asked him. The Girls said they never knew he could be so attentive; he confessed he never knew it himself. Now? Naomi would say, growing angrier with every kindness. Why not before?

He didn't even mind Naomi's digs. How sick could she be, he'd say, if she can still get so mad at me?

Half of the time he couldn't hear her anyway; his hearing had started to slip long before Naomi's illness. He'd insisted it hadn't and for years he'd refused to get a hearing aid.

It's this family, he told us. If you'd all speak clearly, I could hear fine. I don't have trouble with anyone else.

Then there was a slight car accident—he hadn't heard the horn of the other car warning him before he clipped its fender—he gave in and got a hearing aid. Most of the time he forgot to wear it.

I wouldn't mind the hearing, Naomi said, he never listened anyway. But sometimes I think his memory's going too. Her patience for him was wearing thin.

"Yes?" he asked Naomi, "did you say you wanted ice?"

"No, no, no," she practically screamed.

He looked disgusted. "What are you doing to yourself? Didn't I tell you not to talk?" Hersh turned to me. "I don't remember, did she say she wanted me to get the nurse?"

"No," I said. I'd learned to speak to him in a voice so loud it bounced off the walls. Sometimes after a day with him, Billy and I would forget to lower our voices and we'd boom at each other until our throats were sore.

"Fine," he said. "Then why don't you girls talk while I read the paper." He put on his little black reading glasses.

"You rest too," I told Naomi. "If you need anything, I'll be here."

"Great," Naomi said, "just great. We're paying three nurses to take care of me and they're never around. Leave it to your father to hire nurses who never show up."

"Then do you want something? Do you want me to get the nurse?"

"No. I want them here because they're supposed to be here. Oh, what difference does it make?" She closed her eyes, her hands shook with rage.

"I've been thinking about moving," I said, "I need a

bigger place. When you're better, you'll have to come help me decorate it."

"A bigger place?" she said. "Alone?"

"You always said you thought my apartment was too small. And if I have more room," I said, "there'll be a place for you to stay when you visit."

"I'll believe it when I see it," she said. "I'd rather see you married," she couldn't resist adding.

Hersh's head fell back, his mouth dropped open, his glasses slipped to the side of his face. He made so much noise snoring, I didn't hear Billy come in.

"Looks very familiar," Billy said.

Naomi opened one eye. He leaned down to kiss her forehead.

"You too," she mumbled, half awake, "with the old jacket. What is it, a pact between the two of you to never make me happy?"

"She sounds the same to me," Billy said.

"Hello, hello, hello," a woman in a white uniform sang as she came in the room. She wore a button on her collar that said, "Fight germs, wash your hands." "I'm Hannah," she said and held out a freshly scrubbed hand, "and you must be the children I've heard so much about. But she hardly looks old enough to have children your age." I thought I saw Naomi smile.

Hannah wrapped the blood-pressure cuff around Naomi's arm. "Have you spoken to her yet?" She worked a thermometer in between the tubes in Naomi's mouth.

"A little," I said, "but I think she wants to sleep."

"Now none of that," Hannah said to Naomi. "You've got company, dear, and we must get you looking nice for them. See how nice she looks already in her pretty pink jacket?" While Hannah talked she pushed the button to change the bed's position; she had Naomi sitting almost straight up. Naomi still hadn't opened her eyes.

"There now," Hannah said. She stopped the bed when it was at right angles. She pushed the pillow back over Naomi's stomach. "You want to hold onto that, dear. See, we like to keep her sitting up to get the circulation going. She shouldn't be sleeping too much. It isn't good for you, is it? What was it Hannah told you? That's right. We get the circulation going, then all those nasty scabs will disappear, won't they? And you want to freshen up for your company, don't you?" Hannah fiddled with the tubes, checked her watch, took the thermometer out, wrote on her chart, and kept talking. "Mr. Asher's asleep, I see. Well, we'll just let him rest. But if you two will excuse us, we've got work to do. You can come back in half an hour. Then we'll be looking our best, won't we?"

"Can't you let her sleep?" Billy said. "She looks so tired."

"She's just playing possum with us, isn't she?"

"Yes," Naomi said quietly. She licked her lips. "Could I have some ice? My mouth is so dry."

"See, what did I tell you? Next thing you know, she'll be wanting an extra-dry martini to go with it. You've got to keep your eye on this one—she's sharp. Never seen anything like it. One extra-dry martini coming up." Hannah rubbed an ice cube over Naomi's lips. "And if you two are going downstairs, I'd like *The New York Times*. Your father and I fight over the crossword puzzle. Looks like he got to today's before I did."

"That's because you weren't here," Naomi said.

"See what I'm telling you? She's sharp. And where do you think Hannah was? You think I was out in the halls flirting with the doctors? I was getting more towels and fresh sheets. I called for them, but no one brought any, so

I had to go get them myself. She doesn't like it if I'm gone for more than a minute." Hannah winked at us. She started stripping the bed around Naomi and kept talking. Billy and I left the room.

The lounge near the elevators was the only place where patients and guests were allowed to smoke; a blue-gray cloud hung over the aqua furniture, the windows were covered with dirt. Mrs. Leonard, a patient we'd met last visit, was still in the hospital. We used to run into her in the lounge, chain-smoking three cigarettes before she'd return to her room. Always three. Three's my lucky number, she said.

She walked holding onto a metal pole with a plastic bag on it attached to her arm. She'd walk and wheel the metal pole around the ward three times a day. Three times she'd circle the floor, then stop in the lounge to smoke three cigarettes. She was nearly as tall and as skinny as the pole she pushed around. Someone told us she either had leukemia or lupus; her doctor was keeping her in the hospital so she could gain weight. Who can gain weight on hospital food? she asked everyone she met as she made her rounds.

Mrs. Leonard sat between a thin teenage boy and a heavy woman with white hair. They were eating out of a big box of Kentucky Fried Chicken. They had paper spread out for the biscuits and butter and coleslaw. Mrs. Leonard recognized us. "I heard your mother was back," she said. "I'm sorry. This is my family. We're getting a head start on Christmas. My boy, Tom, and my mother, Mrs. Johnson. Forgive me, I don't remember your names."

Billy introduced us and Mrs. Leonard invited us to join them. Her mother poked her in the ribs. "What'd you do that for? Here you are skinny as a rail and you go offering your dinner to folks fat as sausages."

"Thank you anyway," Billy said, "we're not hungry."

A man with skin as gray as his flannel robe padded into the lounge.

"George," Mrs. Leonard said, "what you doing out of bed? I thought I heard them tell you to stay put."

He waved his hand at Mrs. Leonard. "Don't listen to them. I stay in bed and I get sick. I can't stay in bed anymore. I came in here a healthy man and now look at me. The longer I stay, the sicker I get."

A nurse came in right after him. "Come on, Mr. Grafman, you know you're not supposed to be out of bed." She took him by the arm and led him out the door.

He kept his head turned back toward Mrs. Leonard. "Go figure. All the young ones are after me. They're always trying to get me into bed. It's shameful. How old are you, sweetheart? You shouldn't be chasing an old man around, you should get someone your own age."

"Help," I said to Billy, "get me out of here."

"Take it easy," he said. "It's going to be all right."

"No, it's not. Now he tells me she could go on like this for a week. Billy, I don't think I can stay here a week."

"We'll manage." He gave me the smile that showed the whole space between his front teeth. We'd discovered we could fit three maraschino cherry stems, two pretzel sticks, or a Cheese Tid-Bit split sideways into that space. He liked it so much he wouldn't have it fixed. For a while he'd let his moustache grow long enough to cover it; now he kept his moustache trimmed.

Billy took out two bags of M&M's; I could always count on him to carry a supply of comfort food. "Care for some lunch?"

"How many have you had so far?"

"Just a bag and a half. I'm trying to cut down."

"Are you stoned?"

"Miserably straight."

"Then let's go get some coffee."

Across the room Mrs. Leonard whispered with her mother. She stood up and wheeled her pole over to us. "There really is enough food here if you want to join us. My mother didn't mean to be rude. She's only trying to take care of me. You know how mothers are."

"Thank you," I said, "but we need to get out for a few minutes."

"If I see your father, I'll tell him where you went." When she sat down with her family, her mother handed her a biscuit with butter melting down the sides.

4

"No food, no children, no change," read the sign on the glass door of the gift shop. "Sounds like us," Billy said. He took a ten-dollar bill from his parka. "Today," he said, "I'm going to make medical history."

Billy was the one who saw every rule as a personal challenge. Grim ignored them, Sharon enforced them, and I was still trying to figure out exactly what they were, but Billy went to battle whenever someone told him no. Each time we visited the hospital he tried to get the unpleasant woman who worked the cash register in the gift shop to break a ten-dollar bill. I waited outside the shop; he hadn't won a round yet.

A familiar-looking man and woman were filling out forms at the admittance desk. The man kept saying, "Would someone please take her upstairs? The contractions are thirteen minutes apart."

"We've called for a wheelchair," the admittance clerk said, her voice as flat as that of most of the other people who worked there. No shred of sympathy, no sense of urgency. "When you've completed these papers, we'll take her right up to maternity."

The pregnant woman shifted her weight; when she clutched her stomach, I could feel my own muscles contract. She saw me twitch.

"Beth?" she said, "is that you?"

"Ellen?" I said. I hadn't seen Ellen Silverman since high school. I didn't recognize her all puffed up so that even her nose, which had been carefully shaped and pared down by a New York doctor, looked large again. I'd heard she'd married Frankie Mariano, her tenth-grade boyfriend, and her parents had had a fit. They'd gotten over it when Ellen and Frankie joined the group of people I grew up with who didn't move away. Some bought houses on the same block as their parents, others moved one town over. Their lives and their parents' lives still overlapped and intertwined; Ellen was having her baby in the hospital where both of us were born.

I hugged her from the side, afraid of bumping into her large belly.

"You haven't changed a bit," she said.

"But look at you," I said. She was sweating through her makeup, the smudged mascara gave her raccoon eyes; the damp hair around her face was starting to curl. "This is just incredible." I had an urge to touch her stomach; I couldn't stop staring at it. "Is it your first?" I said. "Aren't you scared?"

"More like relieved," she said, "it's my last." She took a couple of deep breaths and checked her watch. "We have two boys already. I'm the only one dumb enough to go for a third. Frankie wants a girl. What about you? How many?"

"None," I said. I was imitating the rhythm of her breathing, starting to feel a little anxious myself about the time. "I'm not married," I said; coming between deep breaths it sounded rushed, almost apologetic.

Frankie finished the forms. "Now," he said, "would you please take my wife upstairs?"

"The wheelchair's on its way," the admittance clerk told him.

"I'm okay," Ellen said to him. "Besides, Beth is here, you remember her, don't you?"

"Yeah, sure," Frankie said. He looked older, too. "How's it going?"

The orderly arrived with the wheelchair, but Ellen kept standing.

"Listen, El," Frankie said, "we really don't have time."

Ellen leaned over and kissed my cheek. "You always were smarter than me," she whispered. Then she sat down.

"Good luck," I said. "I'll stop by tomorrow."

Billy was smiling and counting out single dollar bills. "A little charm," he said. "A little talent. It's all in knowing how to ask."

"You bought a newspaper," I said. "Didn't you?"

"But not until I tried to make her give in without it." He pulled *The New York Times* out of his parka.

"I just saw a friend from high school on her way to have a baby," I said.

"Why?" Billy said.

"I don't know, but I think it's got me depressed."

"There's only one cure for that," he said. "Lunch."

• • •

Michele Orwin

What I will never get, Jim said when we were on our way to New Jersey for Passover, is why every time we see your family, it's always got something to do with a big meal.

We'd only been married two months. That undercurrent of contempt I heard in his voice had to be in my imagination. He was just curious, not critical.

I guess it gives us something to do, I said.

But it's always so heavy, he said. It's a good thing I've brought something along to make it go down a little easier. He patted his pocket where he kept his dope. Ten joints in a hand-tooled leather case he'd made when he was into leather work.

In my parents' house? I said. I was still worried about the two of us sharing my room, sleeping together in my bed. When we were living together and visited, we always slept in separate rooms. Marriage seemed beside the point.

You don't give them enough credit, he said. They know what's going on. They'll be fine.

You didn't at your mother's.

We had made our first pilgrimage to his home a week earlier for Easter; until we were married, his mother wouldn't let me in her house. When she finally did, she treated me like an unwelcome guest.

Every Easter his mother continued to dye eggs and set out baskets with green grass and chocolate bunnies for her three grown sons. In the morning, Jim and his two brothers had to hunt for the eggs she'd hidden before we could have breakfast.

I sat in the living room and read the paper. I sat in the only comfortable chair in his mother's house. I sat, without knowing it, on two sky blue eggs and cracked them. It ruined the hunt for everyone, no one could win fairly with two eggs out of the game.

His mother served pancakes but refused to look at me. I apologized. I cleared the table. I offered to do the dishes, but she wouldn't speak.

Let it be, Jim said. Sometimes she can go on like that for days.

Then roll a joint, would you? I don't think I can handle this.

Here? Jim said. Not a chance.

When Jim's mother and brothers returned from church, we sat down to dinner. Jim's brother, Patrick, said it was a sign from God that I would get pregnant soon. I would have two boy babies. It had come to him during the service.

Then Jim's mother relaxed. Of course, she said. Yes, I'm sure you're right.

Jim squeezed my hand. Can't argue with God, he said. We'll do our best.

I kicked him under the table. We'd agreed not to have children until we knew for sure the planet would be safe. Until the war in Vietnam was over. How else could we justify bringing a child into the world?

You copped out, I said later.

Peace, he said. I was just trying to make peace.

A week later, Jim and I were still fighting. We'd declared a truce for the Passover visit to my parents, but the long ride home was wearing us both down. The shocks in Jim's old VW were shot and I was growing weary watching the mudguards on the trucks that kept passing us. I didn't like the way he insisted I have the exact change ready for him ten miles before the toll booths. And I was starting to resent how proud he was about making the whole trip without stopping.

Don't we need gas? I said. We were closing in on home much too quickly. I didn't want to get there too early.

I was only going because of Billy, I hadn't seen him in almost a year. But Billy wouldn't be getting in till around six. Sharon and her family might be the only ones at the house. Aren't you hungry? I said.

That's what I mean, Jim said. Your family's always into food.

We passed a sign warning us the next stop wasn't for thirty-three miles. Just coffee, I said. And a bathroom.

Only if you really can't wait, he said.

I nodded in time for him to make the turn off.

I wish you wouldn't drink coffee, Jim said, after we were seated in a booth. It sets you more out of synch than you already are.

Good advice, I said. I told the waitress coffee and a sugar doughnut.

Jim ate raw cashews. He had a cup of hot water with a lemon wedge.

I won't have to do anything, will I? Jim said. Like ask questions? Don't you all sit around and ask questions at this thing?

I'm sure the only questions anyone will ask us are, When are we going to have children, when are you going to convert? The answer, I said, is, Not yet.

Babe, he said, I'll do whatever you want.

He let me carry our suitcase into the house. We'd fought before over his trying to take care of me.

He makes you carry the suitcase? Hersh said. I've never heard of such a thing. He turned to Naomi. She's carrying the suitcase, he said.

It figures, Naomi said. She kissed Jim hello. What are we going to do with her?

Keep her barefoot and pregnant, Jim said. That and keep her out of the kitchen.

I took the bag up to my room and threw it on the bed. I wouldn't open the door when Jim knocked.

Come out now, he said. Just for a minute. Just to see what I've got.

Never, I said.

Then you're moving back with your folks?

Never that, either, I said.

I heard him go downstairs. He called once more from the landing. Come out and see what I've got for you. I promise you'll like it.

It was Billy with a moustache that grew down into his beard and a beard long enough to rest on his chest. Hair to his shoulders, a guitar under one arm and a pale, delicate girl under the other arm. Mireille, he said, my sister, Beth, and her husband, Jimbo. My only family. She's French, he said, but she speaks English better than I do.

She probably writes better than you do, too, Naomi said. It's been six months, we didn't know where you were.

We were looking for America, Billy said.

I know you'll want to wash up, Naomi said. Maybe shave, get a haircut, change your clothes, do something to yourself before dinner?

We're fine, Billy said. We washed up at the bus station before we came up here.

It's getting so you can't tell the boys from the girls, Hersh said. Your hair's long, hers is short; Beth's carrying suitcases and Tim's cooking dinners.

Jim, I said.

Who can tell the difference? Hersh said.

Michele Orwin

Sharon and Peter, Jessica and Justin, arrived with two booster seats, one Port-a-Crib, a shopping bag full of toys, a tin of plain macaroons and a bottle of apple juice. Peter and Justin were the only ones in jackets and ties.

I've never seen a tie that small, Jim said to Justin, How often do you get to wear it?

Tell Uncle Jim you wear it whenever you go out to dinner, Sharon said. She only looked at Jim's work shirt long enough to ignore it. Tell Uncle Jim that's what big boys wear.

Pretty neat ventriloquist act you got there, Justin. Am I wrong or is your mom trying to tell me something?

Juice, Justin said.

Please, Sharon told him. Juice, please.

Juice, please, Justin repeated.

You got it, Jim said. He picked up Justin and carried him into the kitchen.

He seems to like children, Naomi said.

Just as friends, I told her.

Jessica sat on Billy's lap and played with Billy's beard.

You don't have fleas or ticks in there, do you? Sharon said.

Peter poured himself a drink and left the room.

Mireille, Billy said, this is Sharon. You speak better than she does, too.

Well, Hersh said, it's so nice to have my family all together again.

Naomi had stopped having a real Seder after both of Hersh's parents died. She preferred to serve a simple meal. Her only concession to ritual was the extra glass of wine she kept out for Elijah.

Jessica and Justin were placed at the end of the table. Jim and I were seated next to them. It's good practice,

Naomi said. Jessica kept handing me the food she didn't want to eat. Justin tipped his apple juice over onto Jim's lap. Sharon said he was naughty and wouldn't be allowed to stay at the table if he did it again. Peter said for Sharon to keep on eating, he'd take care of it. He took Justin out for a walk. Jim excused himself, said he'd just go up and change. Billy said he'd go with him, he might have a pair of jeans Jim could wear. Jim winked at me and patted his pocket. Billy smiled at Mireille.

Naomi told Anna to take away the soup and serve the main course. Everyone would be back soon enough. Jessica handed me a grape she'd had in her mouth but didn't want to eat after all.

How long has it been, Hersh said, since we've all been together for a holiday?

Five years, Sharon said.

More like ten, I said. We're still not all together. Grim isn't here.

Then next year, Hersh said, we'll do it right.

I wouldn't count on it, Sharon said. Getting up here with the children was hard enough this time.

Jessica had her thumb in her mouth and all her food on my plate. She made me promise I'd hold her dolls so they wouldn't fall asleep during dinner. Then she climbed in my lap, too, and went to sleep. I was afraid if I moved I'd wake her. Food came and went and I didn't touch it. Billy and Jim, stoned but passing for straight, divided up my servings. Peter poured himself another drink and returned to the table with Justin, who went to sit with Mireille.

It's so quiet, Hersh said. I remember the way it used to be in my house—so much noise, so much tumult. All those children, all that food. Doesn't anyone talk in this family?

I like it this way, Peter said. Peter was the quietest man

I'd ever met. But he's a devoted husband and a good father, Naomi always said about him. If you want conversation, you turn on the television.

Yes, Mireille said, this quiet is good.

Maybe we'll have more children soon, Naomi said. She smiled at Jim. Jim grinned right back.

She looks kind of nice with a child in her lap, doesn't she? he said.

My leg had gone to sleep, my thigh was getting damp from where Jessica's diapers must have leaked through, I was still waiting for a chance to have dinner. Not yet, I said. Remember?

If you say it's because you want to wait till you grow up, Sharon said, I'll leave the table.

She's only twenty-one, Billy said, she's got time.

It's never as much as you think, Naomi said. I hope she does it while I'm still around to enjoy it.

Michael used to say he wanted children. Not a lot, he'd say, just one or two.

Not yet, I'd say.

What about that biological clock? He only asked me once, but it stuck in my mind so that it hurt each time I thought about it.

I think I don't have one, I told him.

I told Sharon that, too, the day she called, because Naomi had asked her to have a talk with me. Naomi was concerned, but she was too tactful to ask me herself, why was it, she wanted to know, I wasn't married and busy producing grandchildren? Did Sharon know if there was some problem? Would she be kind enough to ask?

Despite the way you act, Sharon said, you are not getting any younger. There are complications for women your age, she explained to me. It may take you years and even then you might have a malformed child.

I know, I said, I really do.

If you really understood, Beth, she said the way she usually did when she felt the need to question my competence, then you wouldn't postpone it any longer.

I'm not postponing, I'm just not sure.

Someone's got to tell you this, I'm just sorry it has to be me. But with the way you treat Michael, you'll be lucky if he stays around. If I were you, she said, I wouldn't count on finding anyone else, either. I'm not the only one who thinks this, by the way.

I knew that too. Naomi had gone over the facts of life with me more often since I'd passed thirty than she ever did when I was a child.

I've got a nice life, I said.

But you don't have a family.

I called Michael at work and told him about the talk with Sharon. He brought home red tulips; he told me there was no hurry. He said he was sorry for adding to the pressure.

He was being kind; I was feeling cranky. I was mad at someone, but I wasn't sure who, and there was that comment about the biological clock still pressing on a nerve. If you really want them, I said, I bet what's-her-name's not too old.

Probably not, he said. I guess I forgot to ask her.

5

The coffee shop was part of the new wing of the hospital, built on donations and dedicated to the memory of Rachel Zuckerman, first president of the Women's Auxiliary. It was one of those gloomy modern rooms with dark brick walls and a low ceiling punctured by fluorescent spots. Molded fiberglass chairs were scattered around small white tables; napkins littered the floor near the microwave; machines peddled food on three sides.

"Now this place," Billy said as he brought two chairs over to a nearly clean table, "is depressing. It reminds me of Las Vegas."

"One of us has had a misspent youth," I said. "To me, it looks just like my dorm."

Billy fed his singles into the dollar-bill changer. He filled his pockets with change and accosted the sandwich machine. "I'd like a few minutes to look over the menu," he told the ValuVendor. He pushed the buttons to make the sandwiches swing around. The ham was beige, so were the bologna and the liverwurst, the roast beef was brown. The Swiss cheese was yellow, the American cheese orange. "They've got a pretty interesting assortment today," he said, "beige and yellow or orange and brown. You want one?"

"I couldn't."

"Most days, neither could I. But I was thinking about ham and cheese on a roll. Come look, it's not too bad."

"I'll pass. But if you hit a cherry vanilla yogurt, play it for me, okay?"

"That'll be one E19," he said to the machine, "and if you don't mind, we'll take a G3. Bingo."

"Peach," I said. "You hit the wrong button."

"Oh, shit. I'll get another. I was going to get a box of Junior Mints anyway." Sweet William, I used to call him, because he ate candy when he was upset. Billy, I called him still, though at thirty-four he preferred to be known as Bill.

"Don't bother," I said, "I'm not hungry."

"It helps not to be hungry when you eat this stuff." He squeezed mustard out of a plastic packet onto his roll. "Make sure no one nabs this while I get us some coffee."

"Miss," Billy said to the CoffeeCanteen, "we'd like two extra light, one with sugar, one without." One cup landed crooked and half the coffee poured out of the machine and down the drain. "That does it," he said, "I won't leave a tip."

"I don't blame you, the service stinks."

"You're not actually eating in this place, are you?" Sharon

had arrived. She carried a leather flight bag, she wore her silver fox.

"Well, no," Billy said, "we're waiting for the main dining room to open up. Unless you'd prefer something else. I hear there's a great little buffet brunch by the pool."

"Damn," I said, "I forgot to pack my bathing suit."

"I'm sure you find each other very funny." Sharon looked around for a chair, found one, and waited for someone to bring it to her.

"Pull up a chair," Billy said.

She started to slide one toward the table when Hersh came into the coffee shop.

"Darling." He hugged her. "I'll get that for you." He brought two chairs over and hugged her again. "I'm so glad you're here. I was starting to worry."

Sharon eyed me. "I told Beth I'd be in around one. It was the earliest I could get away. How is she?"

"You won't believe it." He pulled three dollar bills from his pocket. "Beth, get me one of those ham-and-cheese sandwiches. Bill, I'll take a coffee, light. Oh, and a package of cookies, I don't care which kind. Sharon, are you hungry?"

"No. Just coffee will be fine. Black."

"There'll be two more joining us," Billy told the coffee machine. "Yes, thank you and two refills. Hang on a sec, Bether, I want to make sure you get the right sandwich. They've got one in there that's kind of beige with a green stripe. I wouldn't trust that one." He made the sandwiches dance around once more. "There you go. Play E16 and you've got yourself a winner."

"This is how you serve it to me?" Hersh said. "You don't even warm it up and put mustard on it?"

"I'll take care of it." Billy was out of his seat before I

could move. "Just keep breathing deeply," he whispered in my ear, "and you'll be fine."

When Hersh finished eating he rested his head in his hands; then he sat up, wiped his eyes, filled his pipe, and leaned back in his seat. "Now listen, children, I'll go over this again when Grim gets here, but there are a few things we have to get straightened out right away." He took a piece of paper out of his pocket and read to us from his list. "I've got the name of a rabbi to call and I've talked to people who've been through this already. Beth and Sharon, you two will have to pick out her clothes. You know what she has. Find something she'd like. You'll have to do that tonight and bring the clothes with you tomorrow. We won't have much time once it happens, so we'll need the clothes here."

Well, clothes, yes of course, I thought, but I wasn't sure why she needed them.

Hersh went on, "You all have something to wear, I take it. And Sharon, are Peter and the children going to come up?"

"It all depends." She shrugged off her coat, little silver-fox tails skimmed the floor. "Bill, would you bring over another chair? It all depends on which day. If it's the day after Christmas, then there's no problem. Peter's working the rest of the week and the children have their own plans. Any other day's not going to be easy for me, either. This really isn't a good time for any of us to get away."

"Wait a minute," Billy said, "what are we talking about here?"

"You know damn well what we're talking about," Hersh said.

"I believe he was being serious," I said.

"And I believe he was being a smartass." Hersh looked

at the clock over the candy machine. "Now listen to me, it's almost two o'clock, that means tomorrow is out—there won't be enough time. We'll figure on Monday."

Sharon checked her own watch. "It's only one-fifty," she said. "I wouldn't rule out tomorrow. Peter's father went in the middle of the night and we were still able to have the funeral the next afternoon."

"How can you say that?" Billy said. "She's sitting up, she's talking."

"I'm just going by what the doctors tell me," Hersh said, "and they say it could be any time."

Billy said, "I don't believe it."

"All you're doing is upsetting me. We'll talk about it later." Hersh left the room.

"He's right, you know," Sharon said. For as long as I could remember, Sharon had claimed the privilege of being the only one to know when Hersh was wrong. When the rest of us disagreed with him, she was always able to show us why he was right. When she disagreed with him, he was absolutely, unforgivably at fault. "At this point, denial won't work," she said. "His way of coping is by making preparations. You two, obviously, are into regression."

Before she'd settled on law, she'd played around with psychology. We were still her unwilling subjects. She intimidated us with her vocabulary, then she tortured us with interpretations. Though what she said was rarely accurate, it was the way she said it that usually hit us hard. We assured each other she didn't see clearly enough or listen carefully enough to see through us. We agreed she didn't even have the gift of understanding herself. But there was something in her delivery that got to us every time.

Billy sat with his elbows on the table, his fists pressed to his cheeks. I rubbed his arm.

"Why don't you go on up and see her," I said to Sharon. "Let me stay here with Billy. He's upset too."

"I was on my way," she said.

I found Sharon in the ladies' room on Naomi's floor. She stood in front of the mirror with her tongue out; she pulled at her lower eyelid. "God, the lighting in here makes everyone look sick."

"Have you seen her yet?"

Sharon combed her short straight hair and put on lipstick. "I wouldn't dare walk in there without combing my hair first. Aren't you going to do something with yours?" The voice was Sharon's but the words were Naomi's.

I didn't answer her.

"Beth—" Sharon's eyes met mine in the mirror—"this is not the time for you to start acting out. Just comb your hair, for godsakes. In another day or two you can do whatever you want. We all can."

I'd thought my hair was fine; now she'd convinced me it wasn't. I tried to fix it, I put on lipstick, I wiped at the dark circles under my eyes, then gave up.

"Much better," Sharon said.

She hurried down the hall ahead of me, but just as we got to Naomi's room, she stopped. "I think I left my sunglasses. I'll be right back."

"Well, well, look who's returned," Hannah sang to Naomi. She had Naomi sitting up in a mass of plumped pillows, she'd taped a small pink bow to Naomi's fuzzy gray head; she'd painted her cheeks with two dark red streaks of blusher and outlined her mouth with lipstick. "See, doesn't she look pretty?"

"Very," I said and kissed Naomi's cheek. As I ran my

fingers over her head, I took off the bow and put it in my pocket.

"Ready for *Vogue* magazine, that's what I told her," Hannah said. She fiddled with the tubes and dropped the bed back an inch or two. "Well, as long as you've got your company, I'll go have my lunch. Now don't let her go walking around."

"She's so busy all the time," Naomi said, "I can't stand it."

Naomi was funny about the nurses. From the beginning of her illness, they seemed to be her only irritation. She never complained about the operations and the pain, she never complained about the treatments and the medication, but the nurses, and there'd been about ten in the past two years, were never quite right. Molly was the only one who'd lasted. When Molly was unavailable, Naomi was unhappy with anyone else.

I stood near Naomi. With all the new wires there was no longer any room for me to sit on the edge of the bed the way I had on other visits.

"Rest," I said, "I'm here." It was an echo of what she'd said to me when I was six and had to have my tonsils out. Mary had been the one to hold my hand until the doctor told me that if I was a good girl and breathed into the balloon, I could have all the ice cream I wanted when I woke up. Naomi must have changed places with Mary, because she was the one sitting next to me when I opened my eyes. Rest, she'd said, I'm here, she'd told me. Whenever Billy and I rummaged through the past for good memories, it was the scene I thought of first. Now I was the one who'd traded places with Naomi.

"Is she sleeping?" Hersh stopped at the sink to get a glass of water; he drank it, then filled another one.

"Almost."

"Did you eat?" Naomi asked him.

"Sleep?" he said. "No, I wasn't sleeping. I was downstairs getting something to eat."

"That's what I said. I said did you eat?"

"Honey, listen to me. You can't keep straining your voice like that."

"What did you eat?"

Hersh picked up a magazine and started reading.

"She wants to know what you ate."

Hersh didn't answer. I touched his arm. "Please, tell her what you ate."

"I told her I ate, what does she want from me?"

"Never mind," Naomi said, "just leave him alone."

"Is she asleep?" Sharon tiptoed into the room. She walked around the bed and sat on the windowsill.

Hersh took Sharon by the hand and brought her over to Naomi. "She's here," he said.

"I can see that," Naomi said. "And she looks beautiful. Really, she does. Beth, have you seen Sharon's coat? Why don't you have something like that? How are the children? Peter?"

"Fine, everyone's fine." Sharon slipped her hand out of Hersh's. She went back to the windowsill. She got up to clear a place for her coat in Naomi's closet. "You look well," she said while she searched for a hanger. "Go to sleep." She took a book from the stack.

"Sleep? You just got here," Hersh said. "She's not going to sleep while you're here."

"Of course not," Naomi said. "I'm so glad to see you. You've lost weight, haven't you?"

"She didn't eat any lunch," Hersh said.

"No lunch? No wonder you're so thin," Naomi said. My

shoulders tensed as I waited for the comparison that usually followed.

Billy had just come in. He cocked his head and signaled for me to join him outside. "You look like you're starting to fade," he said. "Coming a little unraveled around the edges."

"It's nothing."

"It's Sharon. If it makes you feel any better, I've arranged to have her put to sleep."

Sharon was the villain of our childhood. The house tyrant. I used to tell Billy an evil witch had put a spell on her, that's why she was so mean. One day the spell would be broken and a nicer Sharon would emerge. I still believed, under the surface, she had an untapped streak of kindness. Billy and I argued about it for years.

In the first place, he'd say, we're never going to get under the surface. And in the second place, she'll never be nice.

"Let her live," I said, "she's not my problem."

The woman who cleared the ashtrays and swept the floors was just finishing up in the lounge. She had a dirty rag in one hand and a broom in the other. "See what I mean?" she said. It had to be directed at us, no one else was around. "I tell them what's the use of cleaning here in the middle of the day. It just gets dirty all over again."

"Doesn't it," I said.

"Beats working nights," Billy said.

She was nodding and running her rag around the backs of the chairs. "You watch that John Denver special last night?"

"We missed it," Billy said.

"I'll tell you one thing—" she wiped the table—"he's no Andy Williams."

"Can't argue about that," Billy said.

"But he's better than some shows—" she cleaned the next ashtray—"where they've got girls dancing around in costumes so small, I say to myself, I ought to be a doctor if I'm going to watch people take their clothes off like that." She used the same side of the rag to clean the chair cushions.

"Oh?" Billy said. "Which ones are those?"

"You know what I'm talking about." She tipped the last ashtray into the large trashcan in the hall, then put it back in its stand. "There you go. Now just wait till I'm out of here before you make a mess."

"Are you smoking or quitting these days?" I said.

"I was quitting," he said, "but now I'm smoking."

"Then give me a cigarette."

Billy opened a fresh pack of Marlboro Lights.

"Your hands are shaking," he said. "Okay, one wish."

Mary used to take us outside on the first fall day when the wind blew the leaves off the trees. For every leaf we caught before it hit the ground, we'd get a wish for the next year. We saved the leaves in a cigar box and took them out when we needed them. If we used them up, we'd wish on anything we could find, first stars and candles, eyelashes and chicken bones, the line in the Lincoln Tunnel separating New Jersey from New York. One wish, we'd say, and we'd have to tell it out loud.

"It's silly," I said.

"They're the best kind."

"Just once I want her to tell me I look all right," I said. "Even if it's not true. I want her to look at me one time without criticizing me."

"Code Blue, Code Blue, Room 416, Stat," we heard over the paging system. In minutes a flock of interns flew down the hall, their white coats flapping, their charts at their sides.

"It's never going to happen," I said. "Let's talk about something else."

"Good," he said. "Now when I die, if I'm not married, then I want you to be in charge."

"I'm touched."

"I want to be cremated and I want everyone to get stoned. Mix my ashes in with the grass and smoke me."

When we were in college, he'd wanted to be buried in a burlap sack, with a tree, a willow tree, planted over him as a testimonial to the recycled life. He'd written out instructions.

The interns passed us again, rushing in the other direction.

"I hate planning your funeral," I said, "you keep changing your mind."

Sharon drifted in behind the interns. Our big sister was smaller than we were, with bottle-green eyes and Naomi's nose. She was still tan from her vacation last month in St. Bart's. And beautifully dressed; even as a child she was considered well groomed.

Because she never talked, but only lectured, because she considered anyone who disagreed with her to be not only wrong, but also ignorant, and because she'd always been the preferred daughter, being around her made me edgy.

"Have either of you got any aspirin?" I said.

"Let's see." Billy emptied his pockets of red and blue and green and white and yellow pills. He picked out two white ones. "I'm pretty sure they're aspirin."

Sharon watched over the top of her book. "You wouldn't happen to have any Valium?"

"Never touch it. If you want some though, Naomi's got

drawersful at home. She's been doing tens for years."

"That can't be true," Sharon said. "She's not the type. That woman hasn't had an uncontrolled emotion in her life."

"How many are you on?" he said.

"It's not like that," she said. "I only take them for stress. Not very often. Why am I telling you this, anyway?"

"Then don't," he said. "Meanwhile, my other patient is having a first-rate anxiety attack. Relax, Beth. Take a deep breath. Come on, I'll walk you around and you'll feel better."

"My head hurts, I'm sick to my stomach, it's hard for me to swallow, and I feel like I can't breathe," I said all at once. "Besides, there's no place to go."

"Then we'll just watch the elevators."

Hannah came down the corridor carrying two brown shopping bags; on the top of one was a box of Russell Stover candy someone had sent Naomi. She wore rust-colored boots that came to her ankles and a handmade scarf with uneven stripes.

"Going home to wait for Santy Claus," she said.

"Have a nice holiday," Billy said.

"I'll try, but I'll be back tomorrow, same as you."

I looked at her but didn't ask.

"Don't worry," she said, "it won't be tonight. I've seen a lot of people pass on and your mother's not ready yet. The doctors don't know everything. When I go to church, I'll take it up with someone who might know a little more."

"Thank you," Billy said. His voice had gone flat. Now it was his turn to feel the sadness we passed between us, my turn to help him over it.

Hannah let the elevator go without getting on. "She'll be fine tonight, I promise you. She hasn't even started to get fluid in her lungs yet. Trust Hannah, it's not time. Go out and enjoy yourself. Why not?"

"You too."

Hannah looked over at Sharon in the lounge. "That's a strange one in there, isn't she? Doesn't even stay in the room. You know, I haven't seen her kiss your mother. You'd think she was afraid she could catch it."

"She's not really like that," I said.

"That's just her way," Billy said.

"If you ask me," Hannah started. Another elevator opened in front of us and Billy eased Hannah on. He made her squeeze in next to a man on a gurney, his head and hands wrapped in bandages.

It must be difficult being Sharon, Michael said the first time he met her.

We were sitting around her new pool, she was finishing her forty-minute swim.

I never thought of it that way, I said. It's hard enough being her sister.

So much perfection takes its toll, he said.

Ah, but if I just had a little of it.

Sharon climbed out of the pool and sat down with us. She shook her head to dry her hair. If you swam, Beth, she said, you'd lose some of that cellulite on your legs in no time.

I swear, Michael said, before I even had a chance to ask him, I never noticed. Honest, he said, squeezing my knee, I still don't see it.

6

Sharon walked laps around the lounge. "This is ridiculous," she said, "what does he want us here for? We can't do anything. She doesn't want to talk to us." When Sharon was mad her bones stood out, I could see the sharp lines in the base of her neck. "I might as well work, there's nothing else to do. Bill, I left my papers in the room; would you get them for me?"

"Let's all go," I said. "Maybe she's awake."

But Hersh and Naomi were sleeping. Mrs. Bauer, the new nurse, sat by the bed knitting. She had the tiny television set a few inches from her face. She put a finger to her lips to keep us quiet. "Let them rest," she whispered. "It's the best medicine."

"I think I'll stay and see if I can't get some sleep," Billy said. "I was up all night."

Sharon had already taken her bag to the lounge. I wandered down the hall, looking in open doors at the other patients; most of them were watching television. It was that long part of the afternoon when the sky went dark early and everyone waited for dinner to take up the time until visiting hours. The nurses talked on the phone to their friends. The doctors were back in their offices.

I read the instructions on the wall for what to do in case of an emergency evacuation. I passed Mrs. Leonard circling the hall on the way back to her room. I stopped to watch Sharon through the lounge window.

She had her files out on the table; she sorted through them, made notes, then spoke into her small tape recorder. I tried to pretend she was a stranger. She and Grim had always seemed like they were part of another family, anyway.

We're classic overachievers, she'd told me. You're lucky you never had that problem.

When it came to the two of them, Naomi and Hersh were fickle but proud; whichever one achieved the most, that one became the favorite. Grim had gone to Harvard, he was a professor, he published articles. But Sharon had gone to law school, been made a partner in her firm. Grim had three children, Sharon only two. But Sharon had never been divorced. Grim evened the score by marrying Lonnie last May, then Sharon moved into a new house in August; it was too close to call.

Sharon looked up to see me watching her from the hall. "Come in," she said, "I won't bite."

She had, once, and I'd never forgotten it. We'd been playing hide-and-seek at the house down the shore. The two kids from next door were found right away, Billy'd been caught, Grim had quit. I was the only one still out.

Waiting for Next Week

I was crouched behind a bush when Sharon sneaked up and bit my back.

She even broke the skin, said Mary, our nurse and protector, when I presented my wound.

Did not, she said, there's no blood.

But why did you bite her? Mary asked.

Because, she said, I didn't win.

Sharon put the tape recorder back in her bag. "This is absurd," she said, "or don't you see what's going on? Naomi's doing what she's done to us all her life, controlling us till the very end. Anyone else would have killed themselves, but not her. She has to keep all of us gathered around her. How could anyone be so selfish and manipulative?"

"You're not serious," I said.

"Completely. I wouldn't put it past her to die while I'm the only one in the room just to screw up the rest of my life."

"Sharon, I don't think she's got this all planned out."

"But you've always been naive," she said. She drew hatch marks on the legal pad in front of her.

The day after Naomi was diagnosed, Sharon called me at work.

You know what this means, don't you? We're next.

That's not true, I said. That's not what her doctors said. Even Roz had told me I had no reason to worry.

I'm sorry to be the one to tell you, Beth, but we don't stand a chance. Already I've discovered several small lumps. My doctor says they're cysts, but that's how it starts. You probably have them too.

But I don't.

Then you will. You really ought to see a doctor immediately. Ignoring it won't keep it from happening. I don't want to scare you, I'm just telling you for your own good.

Thank you, I said, but I'm fine. We're not the ones who are sick, Sharon. She is.

For now, Sharon said. If I were you, I'd make an appointment right away. And listen, don't say anything to them about me. Please. That's all I need.

I called Billy. It's not that I'm worried, I said.

I understand, he said, it's only that you're terrified.

Well, maybe a little, I said.

I think what we've got here, he said, is a basic case of projection. Billy stored psychological terms to use as ammunition against Sharon. He studied the jargon, then practiced on me. Do you remember the school bus? he said.

When Billy and I were four and five and learning to cross the street without Mary, we would get up in the morning and make walking plans for the day. Anna would pack a lunch for us and we'd set off for the park. Down the block, around the corner, we'd wait at the stoplight, then cross the first street. Billy and I would take turns holding up our hands to stop the cars, just in case. Two more blocks, another stoplight, and we'd be at the park.

Mary would follow one block behind; it was the only way Naomi would let us out of the house. We were doing well, we were making progress, we no longer let the lights go through two or three changes before we dashed across the street. Mary called us her brave adventurers. Soon we'd be allowed out alone.

Sharon and Grim, out alone all the time, were so far ahead of us in school, we only saw them when they rushed in at the end of the day to drop off their books and then rushed out. They ate dinner at their friends' houses, or they ate dinner fast, and then they were off in their rooms on the phone or fighting with each other. We never knew what either of them was doing until Sharon decided to try out for cheerleading. Then we heard her kicking and jumping, cheering and clapping for hours. Our parents were sure she'd make it; had she ever not gotten anything she wanted?

But the day of tryouts she overslept. Hersh, who still hovered over her, waited for her and drove her to school. She was in such a hurry when she got out of the car, she ran across the street without looking. A school bus stopped inches away from her. Hersh saw it all. He was going to sue the bus driver, sue the school. He was going to take the whole world to court if the incident had upset Sharon. But Sharon said she was fine. She made the squad; she was voted junior co-captain.

The next day, when Billy and I were on our way out to the park, Sharon stopped us.

I'd be very careful if I were you. You're both going to get hit by a bus someday.

Nonsense, Mary said. There's not even a bus that travels the streets where we go.

They come out of nowhere, Sharon said. I've seen them. They come out of nowhere and they run over little kids. It happens all the time. It's true.

Everything Sharon said was true, she already told us she didn't believe in make-believe.

They're so little the driver won't even see them. He'll run right over them and never stop, Sharon said.

Mary packed our lunch anyway and we set off. When we let the light change four times, she shortened the distance between us and held our hands crossing the street.

About two weeks after that, Grim hid Sharon's special cheerleader's red underpants before the first football game.

If she didn't find them she'd be the only one out there in white cotton Carter's and would probably die of embarrassment. We all knew where he'd put them, even Mary, but none of us ever told her.

Of course, I remember the bus, I said. But what's that got to do with it?

Projection, pure and simple. She's really worried about herself, he said, she doesn't give a damn about you. But she figures if she's got to suffer, you should suffer, too.

For a funny-looking kid, you're pretty smart, I said.

Only sometimes.

Then you don't think I've got cancer?

Now I'm not a doctor, Billy said, but based on the evidence, I think you're okay.

The afternoon was going even slower. I turned on both lamps in the lounge so Sharon could get back to work. I felt safer with Sharon busy; this was the most time we'd spent alone together in years.

"How long are you staying?" I said.

"Don't tell Hersh, but I'm probably going back tonight." She made thick spirals across the page.

"I was thinking I might leave too. Maybe tomorrow and come back Wednesday."

"You won't," she said, "I know you." On a fresh sheet of paper, she sketched a caricature of my profile. She made my chin too sharp.

She spoke with such authority, it seemed possible she might know me, though in the past twenty years, we'd only spent a few days together. Sharon came to Washington once when Justin's teacher told his class that anyone who took a field trip to the nation's capital would receive extra credit.

I was to be chauffeur and tour guide, then, it turned out, babysitter, too.

Sharon and the children arrived on a Thursday. Friday morning Sharon had to leave unexpectedly. She didn't want to ruin everyone else's vacation, the children could stay with me. She was sure they wouldn't be any trouble. At least it would give me something to do.

On Sunday I called Sharon to tell her Justin and Jessica were on the plane home with panda T-shirts and a box of firecrackers, they'd seen enough historic sites to qualify for three years' worth of extra credit, and if they said they'd missed a meal, not to believe them.

She said it sounded like it had been wonderful; she was sorry she'd missed it. She promised she'd send them back to visit soon.

I was going to tell Sharon she knew nothing about me when a woman in a pink flowered housecoat and blue terry slippers walked into the lounge. She had a towel wrapped around her head.

"Oh, what nice girls," she said, "pretty girls. I bet you two are sisters. I'm right, aren't I?" She sat down next to us. "Now, don't tell me, let me guess. You must be the younger one," she said, looking at Sharon. She pulled at the long white hairs growing from her chin.

Sharon shook her head. "If you'll excuse us," she said, and moved her chair closer to mine.

"Go right ahead," the woman said, "don't pay any attention to me." Her stomach growled; she patted it, then belched. "Much better."

Sharon mouthed the words, "Let's move."

I mouthed back, "We can't."

The woman picked up the edge of Sharon's skirt and

rubbed it between her fingers. "Hundred percent wool," she said, "I know it when I see it. I had a hundred percent wool coat once. Bought it at S. Klein's. It was the warmest coat I ever had."

"That's nice," Sharon said. She took her skirt out of the woman's hands.

"I don't have much now, but I've still got my teeth." She opened her mouth and showed us yellow teeth turning in on each other. "My hair's gone though." She unwrapped the towel. "Bald as a cue ball. I tried those ice packs but they didn't work. Sure would like to have your hair," she said to Sharon. "Yours is nice," she told me, "but I look better with my hair short. I'd wear it like that Princess Diana."

"We're trying to have a conversation," Sharon said.

"I'm talking too, aren't I?" the woman said. Her stomach growled again. "Maybe what I've got to say's important."

"I'm sure it is," Sharon said.

"Well, then," the woman said and pulled her chair closer to ours. "You look like you know so much, but I bet you don't know how when a woman gets to be a certain age, the doctors like to start cutting you up. It's the truth. They got my left breast, and one of my lungs, my uterus, and while they were in there, they took out my appendix."

"You should have gotten a second opinion before you let them operate," Sharon said.

"Second opinion? Sugar, I couldn't even pay for the first one."

She massaged her thigh, then hiked up her housecoat to show us her leg. "Fell off the operating table and got a hematoma the size of a coconut. Good thing my husband's not alive to see what's happened to me. Don't even like to have my children around. I tell them they won't have much to bury when the doctors are through. But the little one, he says, 'It's okay, Grandma, you still got your lap.' 'Baby,' I tell him, 'I'll never let them take that away from me as long as you need it.' "

Sharon was busy moving papers around inside her briefcase. She took out one of her business cards and gave it to the woman. "If what you're saying is true, you know you might be able to file a malpractice suit. Call me in a couple of days. There's someone I know who's very good with these cases. Don't worry about the money."

The woman held the card in her hand. "Well, maybe you're not as smart as you look," she said. "It's too late for all that, sugar. Everything they left inside me is so full of cancer, they can't even cut it away anymore. I'd let them, but it won't do any good."

"Oh," Sharon said. I saw a tear slide down her cheek.

"Now look what I've done," the woman said. "I talk too much. Don't waste your tears on me, it could be worse—I could be all alone." She stood up and wrapped the towel around her head. "I can't stay, I got my tray coming and they're giving us Jell-O tonight."

Sharon took out her compact and covered the tear tracks with powder. "It was what she said about being alone," Sharon said. "I was thinking of you."

Mrs. Bauer came to tell us it would be a good time to wake Hersh and get him some dinner. She wanted to take care of Naomi, bathe her, change her dressings.

Hersh slept in the most uncomfortable chair in the room. He claimed he could fall asleep anywhere, then proved it by nodding off in odd places and awkward positions. But try to change anything to make him comfortable and he'd wake up. I took the reading glasses off his nose.

"What?" he said.

"Let's go eat."

"Good idea, good idea." He struggled to his feet; he took his hat and coat from the radiator. "Come, children, kiss your mother goodnight."

I kissed her forehead and ran my hand over her hair. Billy kissed one cheek and stroked the other. Sharon stood next to the bed and blew a kiss. Naomi was too groggy to say goodnight.

"I'll be back," Hersh told Mrs. Bauer. "Have them set up a cot."

"You shouldn't stay," Sharon said.

"How's Chinese?" he said. "I know you children would like that."

The Canton Palace, in the middle of an old shopping center, was the only Chinese restaurant Hersh, Naomi, and all their friends trusted. There were places in New York they'd try on recommendations, but for local Chinese food, there was only one restaurant where they felt safe.

Naomi had been brought up in a kosher home; although she'd broken with it almost completely, she still felt a little sick every time she ate pork, and shellfish made her queasy. For all her sophistication, she liked a place that served a nice chicken chow mein. But Hersh couldn't get enough barbecued spareribs and shrimp in lobster sauce. He adored egg rolls. In all the years they'd been eating Chinese food, they never ordered anything else.

As we walked to our table, Hersh stopped to talk with all the people he knew.

"Christmas Eve always our busiest night," the owner told us. "Where else your people go they don't see decorations?"

Sharon was displeased. "I can't believe," she said, putting down the huge red ten-page menu that offered everything from pu-pu platters to cheeseburgers, "they don't have Szechuan. This must be the only restaurant in the United States that's still serving Cantonese. I hope we can at least get chopsticks. I refuse to eat with silverware."

"Don't start," Hersh said. "Bill, why don't you order for us? You know I'll have the wonton soup, the egg roll and the spareribs. That's all I like anyway. Anything the rest of you want is fine with me."

Billy tried to give the waiter our order, but Hersh kept interrupting, changing dishes, correcting Billy.

The waiter shook his head. "Too much food for four people," he said; Billy had to give our order again.

I began to pour tea for everyone, Hersh's cup first. I judged wrong and tea spread out in a small circle on the tablecloth in front of him.

"I'll pour my own," Sharon said.

Billy picked up the bowl of fried noodles, took a handful and passed them to Hersh along with the hot mustard.

"Cleans out your sinuses," Hersh said every time. "Sharon, be careful not to take too much."

The busboy filled our water glasses for the second time.

A man dressed in tailored casual clothes came up behind Hersh and clasped him on the shoulder. "How nice you have your family with you at a time like this," he said. He had the deep voice and solemn intonation of a rabbi.

"It is," Hersh said, "my only comfort."

"How is she?" The man waved to someone at a table near us.

"Not good. I'm going back tonight. They say it could be any time."

The man was already on his way to greet the people at

the next table. "Well, you've got your family, that's all that matters. Give Naomi my love."

The waiter came back to go over the order one more time. Hersh had turned down his hearing aid and couldn't understand the problem. "It's a simple thing," he said to Billy, "I thought you could take care of it." He adjusted his hearing aid and winced. "I have to keep it off," he said. "All I get is the noise in the restaurant." There was a time when Hersh's hearing was so fine he could pick up every word Billy and I mumbled under our breath.

Sharon played with her soup. She followed the line of dragons chasing each other's tails around her bowl. "I've decided I'm going home tonight," she said. "I'll go back to the hospital with you and catch a cab from there."

Hersh ignored her. "Soup's good," he said. "It's getting so cold out. I just hope it doesn't snow. Then what will we do?"

The waiter set down five covered silver bowls in front of us. He removed the lids.

"You call that fried rice?" Sharon said.

"Pork fried rice, yes," the waiter told her.

"You've forgotten the egg roll," Hersh said.

The waiter took out his pad. "No egg roll," he said.

Hersh looked at Billy. "You're thirty-four years old," he said. "Don't you think it's about time you did something right?"

"I wasn't the one," Billy said, "who made the mistake." He told the waiter to bring Hersh's egg roll.

Hersh passed me his cup for more tea; this time I poured it perfectly.

"It's cold," he said. "I can't drink this. We'll get another pot."

Sharon had her cup to her lips.

"Don't drink it," Hersh told her, "it's cold."

Sharon balled up her napkin and threw it on the table. "That does it," she said, "I'm going to call a cab."

Hersh spoke through his teeth. "Do not make a scene. You're not going anywhere right now. If you want to go back when I go to the hospital, fine. But first you will sit through dinner. That is not asking too much."

They'd played this scene for as long as I could remember. Sharon would threaten to leave, Hersh would order her to stay. When Naomi was around, she'd take over.

He means well, she'd say to Sharon.

But I refuse to be treated like a child, Sharon would insist.

He's your father, he's only trying to help, Naomi would answer. Sharon would still be poised on the edge of her chair, ready to leave. Then Naomi would say, He won't always be here, you know. Someday you'll wish you had someone to take care of you the way he does, but he'll be gone.

Then Sharon would put her napkin back in her lap and sulk for the rest of the meal.

Without Naomi, the scene never ended, dinner seemed to go on forever. The busboy filled our water glasses eight times before Hersh finally called for the check.

"It's only seven-thirty," he said. "If you still want to go back tonight, then come with me and I'll take you to the airport. We'll drop the children off first. But think about it," he said. "I have a feeling you'll never forgive yourself if you're not here at the end."

Sharon went white. Billy and I moved closer to her, but she backed away. "What a sadistic thing to say," she said.

"If you can't stay," I said, "we understand."

"She would too," Billy said.

"Evidently," Hersh said, "you know nothing about your mother but what you choose to see."

"Next year you come back," the owner said as we headed for the door. "Christmas tradition."

A few years ago, Michael and I went skiing over Christmas. He loved steep, snow-covered slopes; I preferred warm, smooth beaches, flat, dry city sidewalks. Even San Francisco gave me vertigo. I couldn't ski.

He told me to picture a quiet country inn, a blazing fire, hot buttered rum, a romantic dinner. He would teach me to ski, he was sure I would love it. Finally I agreed to try cross-country skiing.

But the ski lodge with the fireplace was overbooked; we had to stay at the Holiday Inn with the video games in the lobby. And the only restaurant open Christmas Eve in that part of West Virginia was the Luau Lounge. The hot buttered rum they served turned out to be a warm glass of Bacardi with a film of grease floating on top underneath a parasol. The Polynesian chicken was so sweet we couldn't eat it.

Just tell me, I said, when we get to the part I'm going to love.

The next morning, an unexpected warm front moved in and the heavy snow they'd been predicting came down rain. The fog was so thick we couldn't see the hills. We decided to turn around and go home.

Michael dropped me off at my apartment. He hadn't spoken to me all the way back. If I'd been a better sport, his silence told me, this never would have happened. If that's your attitude, I tried to let him know, without speaking, then let's just forget it. Fine with me, was what I read in his face.

When I finally stopped being angry, when I had started feeling a little guilty, when I began watching the phone, rehearsing how I'd apologize, he came to the door with a bag of takeout Chinese food.

Sitting up in bed later, with the sheets wrapped around us to keep out the cold, dipping into the paper cartons, I had to admit I might grow to like skiing.

All I asked, Michael said, was that you give it a chance.

Running my hand over his shoulder, tracing the curve of his arm, I realized if he hadn't come over, I wouldn't have called.

Stroking his face with the back of my hand, I found one of his long eyelashes curled on his cheekbone. I pinched it between my thumb and forefinger.

I wish, I said, and opened my fingers, you didn't make me feel like I'm always wrong. I blew the eyelash off my thumb.

7

Hersh made us wait inside where it was warm, while he alone went out into the cold to get the car.

Billy had pocketed a handful of pastel mints on his way out of the restaurant; he offered them to Sharon and me.

"No doubt about it," he said. "There really is nothing like spending the holidays with your family."

The second year Michael and I were together, he wanted to have our families over for Thanksgiving dinner.

It'll never work, I told him. I can't cook and have my parents in the room at the same time.

Don't worry, he said. I'll do all the cooking.

But your parents, my parents. They'll talk about marriage, they'll ask about babies. It's difficult enough when

I hear it from you. I'm angry already and it's only October.

Take it easy, he said. It'll be fine.

Michael had a way of relaxing that always made me tense. Just being around him when he was feeling mellow could give me a headache.

Our brothers and sisters, too, he said three days later. We'll invite them all.

Sharon won't come, I said. We don't have wallpaper in the bathroom. We don't have a separate dining room.

Easy, he said. None of that matters. What's important is that we'll all be together. It'll be fun.

Fun? I said. You never sat around our dinner table when we were growing up, otherwise you'd never call what goes on fun. William, sit up straight, don't mumble when you talk. Beth, can't you get the hair out of your eyes? Sharon, what wonderful things have you done today? Grim, how many awards did you bring home? Beth, you don't need any more of that, pass the bowl of potatoes to Sharon, she's looking so thin, isn't she? Please, I said to Michael, I'll do anything, just don't make me sit down to dinner with all of them ever again.

Just ghosts, he said. We'll put them to rest.

Michael had an idealism I admired in his professional life but I found difficult to live with when he brought it home. I didn't want him to change, I only wanted him to work his wonders on someone else.

The problem is, I said to Billy when I called to tell him about Michael's outrageous plans for our Thanksgiving, he came from a happy family.

I know, Billy said. I've met people like that too. They're so well adjusted they make you uneasy. They lack anguish, they're without turmoil. But he was willing to overlook Michael's flaws and he'd be happy to come for dinner.

Sharon was quick to say no, she could not possibly come for Thanksgiving at our apartment, she was having a catered dinner for the partners in her firm.

See, Michael said, things are looking up already.

Grim turned us down, too. There was going to be a big Peace Corps reunion dinner in New York, all his old friends from Mexico, his buddies from the Philippines.

Probably roast up a few dogs with rice stuffing, Billy said to me. He wouldn't dare say that to Grim.

Michael's parents said yes, then they said no, then yes again. It all depended on his sister, Barbara. She was expecting a baby mid-November. If we were having a baby, they would have done the same for us.

You see, I said, I told you it would be like that. Next they'll be asking us about china patterns, silver place settings.

I do love you, Michael said, but I'm not always sure why.

Same here, I said. I don't want this dinner.

Finally, Barbara was scheduled for a C-section two days before Thanksgiving. His parents promised to visit later in the year. His brother, Stan, was living in California, there was never any real chance he'd show up, he was a vegetarian, a budding Buddhist, American Thanksgiving had no meaning in his life as he now lived it.

We were left with Billy and my folks. I was happier complaining about their never coming to see me than I was about having them visit.

I'll invite Sarah for Billy, Michael said.

Sarah? I said. Sarah? I repeated a little louder than I'd meant to.

Young, he said. And walleyed. She doesn't shave her

legs. Her moustache is darker than mine and her eyebrows make one thick line across her forehead.

So what? I said. You don't notice those things.

Conservative, he said. She voted Republican her first time out.

Invite her, I said. Invite anyone you want. I'm going away.

Michael ordered a fresh turkey from Gleason's. No bruises, he told Joe, evidently Michael knew about Thanksgiving. Twenty pounds, he said, would be just right. I'd never cooked a turkey, didn't plan to start.

No one's asking you to, Michael said. You don't have to do a thing.

Michael knew about cranberry relish made with fresh cranberries, he knew about stuffing with sautéed onion and celery, he'd try the water chestnuts some other time. He knew how to make gravy from pan juices.

Billy had come down a day early with a few Thai sticks, a box of colored soaps shaped like flowers he'd picked up for us at the train station, and a change of jeans.

This is infuckingcredible, Billy said as he watched Michael turn the dark gloppy stuff in the bottom of the roasting pan into a thick, smooth gravy.

Michael was putting the sweet potatoes into the oven when Hersh and Naomi arrived. Naomi had picked up a barbecued chicken just in case Michael's turkey didn't work out. She'd had Anna prepare a brisket just in case the chicken wasn't enough.

And where, Hersh wanted to know, was everyone else? Had they driven down for nothing?

Never mind, Naomi said, trying to make up, as she usually did, for Hersh's lack of tact. Beth, why don't you show us around, we'd love to see the rest of your place.

You have, I said. This is it.

Well, at least, Hersh said, you won't get lost.

See, Michael whispered to me, I don't know what you were so worried about—they love it.

Then Sarah showed up, as plain and hirsute as Michael had promised.

Very European, Billy said. He was so high he fell for her right away.

You must be Southern, Naomi said to Sarah. Southern women are always so interesting-looking.

Hersh turned on the television, took over the sofa and stayed there until all the food was out on the table.

You know the funny part is, he said when he sat down with the rest of us, I don't even like football. Can you imagine that?

Hersh had always displayed a fascination with himself he expected everyone else to share. Funny, isn't it, he'd say, but I haven't read the paper in days. Or, do you know, I can't remember the last time I had fish.

What are you talking about? Naomi would say. You just had fish last night.

There, you see, Hersh would answer, that's my point—I can't remember it.

Naomi would roll her eyes and count off on her fingers exactly how many years they'd been married.

They kind of remind me of Burns and Allen, Michael said. In their own way, they're pretty funny.

Give up on it, Billy said to me. The man will never understand certain things.

Michael's turkey was perfect, his gravy a little salty, his stuffing a bit dry; the sweet potatoes were stringy, but we agreed it wasn't his fault and Naomi said perhaps if we had a strainer we could remove the pieces of cork floating around in the white wine.

You know, Hersh said, that's the most I've ever eaten for Thanksgiving.

Michael took it as a compliment. Naomi had the grace not to argue she'd seen Hersh eat twice that much.

As soon as I'd put the coffee on the table, along with an apple pie Michael had bought, Billy asked Sarah if she'd like him to take her home.

So soon? Hersh said. The evening's young. I'll bet it's not even seven yet.

What do you care? Naomi said. You'll be asleep soon anyway.

We're looking at the long face of marriage, Michael, I said when we were alone in the kitchen cleaning up. And I don't like it.

Michael wrapped the white and dark meat separately, he showed me where he put them in the refrigerator. We won't have to worry about dinner for a week, he said.

I've been married before, I said. It didn't work then, it's not going to work now.

Whenever Michael thought I was getting hysterical, he tried to ignore me. The gravy, he said, is in this pitcher.

I will club you with a drumstick, I told him. I will place small turkey bones down your throat. I will stuff congealed gravy in your ears, I . . .

Billy came in to say goodnight. Must be talking about marriage, he said. He punched Michael on the arm. Good luck with her. It won't be easy.

Naomi was right behind him carrying plates I'd left on the table. If I help, she said, we can get this done in no time. You'll just have to tell me where you want me to put everything—there doesn't seem to be much room.

Please, I said, I'll take care of it.

Can't I spend some time with you if I want to? Do you think we drove all this way for nothing?

Either Michael said, How could you be unkind to a mother who's being so kind to you? or else his expression said it for him.

Thanks, I said to Naomi, I could use some help.

Every plate, glass, bowl, pitcher, platter, fork, spoon and knife that had fit on our dining-room table now crowded our tiny kitchen. Every time she brought something in, I had to take some thing else back out.

You know, when you finally get your own place, Naomi said, stacking dishes on one of the kitchen stools, I have some nice china I'd like to give you.

But this is our own place. We have dishes.

Well, what I mean, darling, is when you fix this place up, I'm sure you'll want some nicer things.

This is fixed up.

Well, of course it is. She smiled her tight little smile and with her fingers brushed away the hair that fell into my eyes.

Beth is tired, she said to Hersh. His eyes were just closing as he sat in front of the television. We ought to go so she can rest. It's been a long day and she worked so hard to make dinner for us.

You know, it's the damnedest thing, but I do find myself falling asleep right after dinner lately.

Lately? It's been going on for ten years.

What the hell kind of remark is that? I'm telling you something about myself and you want to turn it into an argument.

Naomi kissed Michael's cheek. It was a lovely dinner, she said. Just lovely. We'll probably grab a bite to eat at the hotel in the morning and leave right from there. You don't have to worry about getting us breakfast. I don't know how you'd manage it anyway, with so little room. She tried once again to brush the hair off my forehead. Next year, she said, you'll come to our house.

Anything you want to tell us before we leave? Hersh said. Any surprises you've been saving?

Naomi's elbow connected with his ribs. When they're ready, she said, they'll tell us.

Then she's putting on weight, isn't she? I thought maybe for a minute, it meant.

What do you know? Naomi said. She's always been like that.

Damnedest thing, Hersh said to Michael as he shook his hand goodnight, but the older I get the more I get my two girls confused.

Michael had the nerve to feel affectionate, he slipped his arm around me while I tried to pretend I was sleeping.

Never again, I said. I will never let you talk me into anything so dreadful.

Tomorrow, he said, when you have the best turkey sandwich of the year, you'll see it differently.

He kept his arm wrapped around my waist and went to sleep.

Two weeks later Naomi called to tell me she had some bad news, at least it looked like it was going to be bad. She'd found a lump in her breast, large already and warm to the touch. She was scheduled for a biopsy immediately.

Please, I said to Michael, help me take back every mean word I said, every awful thought.

Don't worry, he said, I never believed you meant it.

8

Even though Sharon wasn't speaking to Hersh after what he'd said to her in the restaurant, when we got to the car, she automatically took the front seat. Naomi's seat. Billy and I sat in back. Hersh dropped us off before anyone had found a way to break the silence.

Billy and I held onto each other to keep from slipping as we cut a path around the ice patches on the flagstone walk. Wind blew through the maple trees on the front lawn, showering us with leftover snow. The big Tudor house, dark and empty, offered too many hiding places for burglars and ghosts. As children, Billy and I always hated coming home alone.

Whenever we used to enter the house, we'd each grab one of the mahogany walking sticks from the brass stand in the foyer, and tap the sticks in front of us as we lit up every room. Billy inspected the bottom floor, I scouted the top. Together we would case out the basement and attic, the showers and closets.

I flipped the switch to light the front-hall chandelier; unarmed, I headed for our parents' room. Because it had always seemed like the safest room, I used to check there first. But since Naomi's last operation, their elegant bedroom had been transformed into an infirmary. Two Styrofoam heads with different wigs watched me from the dresser. The beautiful porcelain figurine lamps were overrun with boxes of syringes, tissues, straws and plastic cups. Gauze bandages and adhesive tape were mixed in with the cut-glass perfume bottles on the mirrored tray. Just as we'd learned to speak the language of illness, to say without stuttering cancer, chemotherapy, radiation, we'd grown accustomed, too, to the paraphernalia. A bedpan, a walker, a foam seat for the toilet were propped against the love seat. An electric bed was squeezed in between the twin bed frames. Naomi's white nightgown and slippers lay at the foot of the bed. In all the years I'd searched their room for clues, it was the first time I'd come across anything out of place.

I checked the other bedrooms, inside the closets, behind the shower curtains, then I wound my way toward the attic. Billy and I used to stay at the foot of the stairs and call out the lines we'd made up to scare off prowlers.

It's a good thing our father weighs five hundred pounds, we'd shout up into the attic or down into the basement. I'm glad we brought all the police home with us, we'd call.

Silently, I climbed the stairs to what used to be Mary's room, half expecting to find her sitting up in the four-poster bed, smiling, saying, There you are, my angel, I was about to come and wake you. She'd fold back the covers to let me crawl inside with her while the bed was still warm and school was still several years away.

I don't want my children raised by someone else, Michael said the first time I told him about Mary. If you keep on working we'll arrange our schedules so one of us can be home with them.

Michael's mother had been there every day when he came home from school. It wasn't that he ever wanted to talk to her, he just wanted her around. His children, our children, would be entitled to have the best of his experiences, skip the worst, and be spared all of mine.

You really don't understand, I said, there was nothing wrong with it. We loved Mary.

I told him how I'd rush up the stairs and slip into Mary's bed every morning. We'd try to count all the flowers in the wallpaper. Sometimes she'd let me finger the crystal rosary beads draped over the bedpost. For each bead, I'd make a wish. My first wish was always for a million dollars in the bank so I could buy Mary anything she wanted. All Mary wanted, she told me, was a good strong cup of coffee, and a house without too many stairs.

When Billy was old enough to climb out of his crib, he'd join us. We'd sit in Mary's bed and watch her put up her long gray hair with her silver brush, part of the set she kept on a doily on her dresser along with her silver thimble and a pincushion shaped like a strawberry. She'd twist her hair into a bun at the back of her neck and fix it there with huge pins, touch a drop of lily-of-the-valley cologne to her wrists, shoo us downstairs and help us dress. We'd start our day with soft-boiled eggs in china cups, light toast, and milk in a mug with a few teaspoons of her coffee for each of us.

Waiting for Next Week

She taught us to play games with pencil and paper to keep us quiet and out of our parents' hair. She taught us how to sew and how to knit and how to embroider pictures on dish towels, until Hersh found out and told her not to teach those things to Billy. Then she brought us big blocks of modeling clay and showed us how to fashion squirrels and dogs and gray snakes made of clay. She bought Billy a harmonica, and when he learned how to play it by himself, she told our parents it was time they gave him music lessons.

She had a picture of Jesus with a halo around His head over her nightstand, and an ivory figure of Him on a wooden cross above her bed. In the mornings, she liked to talk to Him alone, in the evenings she'd kneel by our beds and we'd pray together. If we ever fell asleep without saying our prayers, we'd wake in the middle of the night and say them twice. I'm sorry, God, I forgot, we'd say. And every night I'd make up my own ending prayer, dear God, please, take care of my family and don't let there be wars and most of all don't let Mary die before me.

She took us to Lord & Taylor's to sit on Santa's lap so we could tell him what we wanted for Christmas and then to her daughter's house to show us the little crèche that her grandchildren made. For Easter she always bought us fancy sugar eggs with windows in them. She promised some day she'd let us go to church with her to light candles. We practiced lighting them in Billy's room.

So tell me, Aunt Rose said during one of her visits as she pinched the baby fat on my cheeks, what are you going to be when you grow up? A dancer? A movie star?

A nun, I said.

This, she said to Hersh, is not so good.

. . .

You see, Michael said, it was confusing for you. Michael liked life easy and uncomplicated. Black and white.

Not really, I said. She lived with us and she loved us. I still wore the mustard-seed necklace she gave me for good luck. Billy still had his harmonica. In a way, she was the best part of our family.

Mary was the one who kept us company when Hersh and Naomi had guests and we had to stay upstairs. She was the one who answered our questions and calmed our fears.

I remembered the time Billy said it wouldn't be so bad if Naomi caught her death of cold and died because then Hersh could marry Mary and she'd get to be our mother. He loved her better, anyway. Sharon told Naomi, Naomi spoke to Mary, and Mary told us we should always love our parents. God wanted it. She wanted it. Billy said he'd pretend, but he wouldn't mean it.

And I remembered the time Sharon told me about babies, and I passed the word along to Billy. I thought it was possible, Billy said it wasn't. It was about the same time someone gave Hersh some birthday presents he wouldn't let us see. We found one in his medicine cabinet, it was a little plastic boy, naked, on a round base. If you put an Alka-Seltzer tablet in the base, then put the little boy in a glass of water, bubbles came out of the hole in his thing. After we saw that, I told Billy to take off all his clothes and stand in the shower, he put an Alka-Seltzer in his mouth, but nothing happened. I told him to try another one. When Mary found us in the shower, Billy was starting to feel a little sick. But is it true, Billy said, about babies? Do they come from the bubbles? Mary explained to us about Mr. Peter for Billy, Miss Virginia for me. She said we should be sure to keep them clean and when we got married we'd learn more. There are secrets and surprises, my angels, she said, when you're old enough you'll know all that you need to.

Billy let it go for a while, then he decided to ask Grim. There was a year or two when Grim was sometimes nice to Billy, he'd let him in his room. Grim said Sharon, for once, was right. He showed Billy a calendar he kept under his mattress, it had a picture of Marilyn Monroe without any clothes on. Billy said Grim had drawn bull's-eyes around the top and a goatee on the bottom.

The next time I took a bath, I sat in the tub long past the point when the skin on my fingers wrinkled. Mary said if I stayed too long after that happened, I'd turn into a mermaid. And what is this? Mary said, when she found me sitting in water already cold. Is it true, I said, that one day Miss Virginia will grow a beard? Well, she said, I don't believe God would let that happen to a girl as lovely as you unless He thought it was right.

And I remembered that one night when Mary stood up from kneeling by my bed, I heard her knees crack. It's just as well, my angel, I'm getting too old for this work, she said. She gave me a backrub and sang the songs that had always put me to sleep. Remember I'll always love you as if you were my very own, she said.

But I am, I said, and hugged her so tight I was afraid she would suffocate.

In the morning when I went up to Mary's room, she wasn't there. Her silver brush, her thick dark stockings, her sturdy black walking shoes, even her lily-of-the-valley cologne were all gone.

I poked Billy awake. Quick, please, hurry up. I pulled him out of bed. We looked all through the house, but we couldn't find her.

How could you do this to me? I stamped my foot by Naomi's side of the bed.

Hersh was the one who sat up. It was time, he said, you're too old to have a nurse.

Beth, darling, listen to me, it's better this way, Naomi said, but I'd already left the room.

I told Billy to dress and we sneaked out the back door. We walked the four miles to Mary's house and waited on her stoop. We scratched open old scabs and touched our blood to pledge we'd never go back. Then Mary found us and took us inside. She had us sit with her in her rocking chair while she smoothed out our hair and sang to us. If you don't go back, she said, then I can't come for dinner Friday nights and I've already promised your mother I'd do that.

And for three years, every Friday, she came for dinner and stayed to put us to bed. She was at all our birthday parties and our school plays. She attended each of Billy's piano performances and all of my dance recitals. She was the one we hugged goodbye before we got on the bus for our first summer at camp.

Set the table for Mary tonight, I told Anna, our housekeeper, the Friday after we'd returned from camp.

Anna stopped in the middle of basting the chicken. Mary won't be coming, Bethie. Didn't anyone tell you? She died in July.

I told Billy. We went to my room and said the prayers we'd meant to keep saying, but hadn't. We lit a candle. Then we made a pact we wouldn't speak to anyone ever again. We kept it for five days and no one noticed.

I am sorry, Michael said, but it won't be like that with us.

There's no point in arguing about this, I told him. I still

don't know if I want children. I'm not ready yet to get married.

I want both, he said, and held up his hand to keep me from interrupting, and I want them with you.

On my way back downstairs I stopped in Naomi's room again. I hung the nightgown on the hook behind the bathroom door. I put her slippers in her closet. I knew she'd be upset if she found out they'd been left lying around.

9

There was a fireplace in the living room, but like the room itself, it was rarely used. Naomi kept an antique clock on the mantelpiece, a pair of silver candlesticks, an onyx box. But she and Hersh, wary of danger everywhere, never considered making a fire; Billy and I were the only ones who took advantage of the fireplace.

When I came downstairs, Billy was hunting for firewood; all he could find were some artificial logs. "It's kind of appropriate, don't you think?" He removed the wrapper that promised an evening of rainbow colors. "Nothing's real around here."

I fiddled with the radio, three stations were playing "I Saw Mommy Kissing Santa Claus"; I picked the one with the least static. Something was wrong with the receiver, but no one had bothered to have it repaired. The stereo was our present to our parents for their forty-fifth anniversary. We'd planned a party, but Naomi's cancer was starting to spread, she'd been hospitalized with a pain in her leg and hip so severe, she couldn't walk.

We'd celebrated their anniversary in the hospital; Hersh had brought a bottle of champagne. With all those tubes in Naomi's nose and mouth, the champagne wouldn't stay inside her long enough to matter.

To forty-five more, Hersh said.

Naomi refused the toast. Make it forty, she said, another forty-five would kill me.

Forty, then.

We raised our glasses. Naomi sipped the champagne and we could see the bubbles race down the tube into the container on the wall.

Forty-five years, she said, while the nurse held the plastic goblet to her lips; I deserve a medal.

I found brandy in the back of the black lacquer bar and poured a glass for each of us. Billy rolled a joint. I took one end of the yellow sofa, he stretched out on the other.

"Forty-five years," I said. "Do you think they were ever happy together?"

"Would you be happy living with either one of them that long?"

"Seriously," I said, "I can't even imagine it. Can you?"

"Forty-five years. I'm having enough trouble trying to picture one." He had the brandy in one hand, the joint in the other. "But I'm starting to think," he sipped the brandy, "that it's getting to be time." He smoked the joint, passed it to me. "And you?" he said as he exhaled.

"Not anymore. I haven't seen Michael in months. Besides, he was too nice. I wasn't prepared to handle nice."

Before I went to college, Naomi sat on my bed for our first and last mother-to-daughter talk.

It's time, she said, you learned the real facts of life. You can't sit around your room and wait for the right man to come along and rescue you, because, darling, there are no Prince Charmings. Absolutely none. What you have to do is find the man you like and turn him into the man you want. If you'd just wear a little makeup and fix your hair, I'm sure you could find someone.

"Ever hear from Jimbo?" Billy said.

"Not a word. I don't even know where he lives anymore."

My second year of college, I found Jim in the library; he caught me searching the stacks with no makeup on and he wanted to marry me anyway. But I never learned how to turn him into what I wanted. After two years he wasn't even what I liked.

Though we'd lived together easily in his apartment, with our mattress on the floor and a couple of orange crates for our books, as soon as we were married he insisted we settle down. He wanted furniture—big heavy sofas with fat arms and upholstered legs, a dining-room table with matching chairs, a stereo with speakers as high as my waist, and an eighteen-inch television set for the living room. All our friends were living in group houses, growing their own vegetables, traveling light. We were shopping in supermarkets, acquiring small appliances. But mostly it was the furniture. My legs became a black-and-blue map of all the pieces I couldn't get used to. Just when I'd stopped banging my shins into our new coffee table, he brought home a record cabinet that caught me at my hip.

One day he surprised me with a new arrangement for the bedroom. I went to sleep that night surrounded by a full Mediterranean bedroom suite, and in the morning I told him I was leaving.

I started over with orange crates, a mattress on the floor, lamps with paper shades, dish towels for curtains, and one plant. I'd waited ten years to try again with Michael.

Meanwhile Billy had tended toward strays. If he couldn't have his piano teacher, he didn't care who he had. He used to bring home out-of-work dancers with delicate faces, skinny arms, and long necks; actresses working as waitresses with wild wavy hair; philosophy majors who'd had nervous breakdowns before they finished their dissertations; women who'd hitchhiked around Europe and lived on communes in New Mexico. He took them in and gave them a place to stay and then let them go.

He'd be better off with a dog, maybe a cat, Naomi said. Dirty as they are, you don't get the same kinds of diseases.

Cheryl, his current girlfriend, was his longest and most serious romance; they'd been seeing each other for two years.

I can't believe, Naomi said when she met Cheryl, he's finally found someone who washes her feet and has a job. There's got to be a catch.

The night after Naomi's first operation, Michael was going to meet me in New York so we could hear Billy play at one of the clubs where he worked. We'd been promising to get there but we never ended up in New York on the right nights.

Don't worry, Billy said, none of the others have ever heard me, either.

Don't pull that sorry stuff on me, I said. I used to listen to you, remember?

Billy practiced the piano because of his crush on his teacher, but he played the piano when he was sad. Growing up, he used to play another hour or two after he'd practiced for four. I'd bring a book down to the living room and curl up in a corner of the sofa while he played. When he'd switch from jazz to classical, I'd know it meant he was so miserable he wanted to be left alone.

I was the only one on duty at the hospital after that first operation; Sharon was in court, Grim was in class, and Billy was in bed with a bad cold. Hersh was in and out of the hospital all day. In the beginning, before it had become a way of life for them, Hersh couldn't stay around the hospital too long without getting jittery. He'd arrive with the intention of lasting the whole day, but after an hour or so he'd remember something he'd have to take care of at the office. He'd leave only to return a little while later and try again to stay the rest of the day.

Naomi said, to be perfectly honest she wasn't even sure she wanted any company. Her stitches pulled, her arm was weak, she had no interest in making conversation. It was just as well everyone was busy, she was too tired to feel slighted.

She was happy, as happy as someone who'd been abandoned by her family could be, that I'd be leaving to meet Michael in New York.

But Billy didn't know if he'd be well enough to play. Michael called to say he wanted to come up anyway. We'd spend a night in the city, stay over at a hotel, top it off with breakfast in bed, and still catch the early shuttle back.

I made the mistake of arguing with him on the phone in Naomi's room; she looked like she was sleeping. I told him not to come, we shouldn't spend the money.

I've been trying to tell you for years, Naomi said, men like women who are charming, gracious.

But, I said.

I know you're going to say it's different now, but let me tell you something—it's not. Women aren't getting any smarter, they're just getting lonelier. In the end, what do you prove?

That I can take care of myself.

Can you? she said. It doesn't look that way to me.

I started to answer, but the nurse came in and asked me to wait outside, she had to give Naomi her medication.

Let him be nice to you, Naomi said before the nurse rolled her over for her shot. What would it cost you to let him be nice?

I called Michael back and told him to meet me in New York.

When I got to Billy's apartment, he was lying in the large loft bed with Shep, his dog, asleep across his feet. Cheryl was in the kitchen making tea. Michael had called from the airport, traffic was bad, he'd meet me as soon as he could.

Think she's a keeper? Billy asked after Cheryl brought him tea and then went back to the kitchen for cookies.

Mary used to show us how to fish in the surf with her when we stayed at the house down the shore. We never caught anything large enough to take home for dinner. The only big one Mary hooked, we weren't allowed to bring in the house. Naomi preferred shopping for food in stores.

Still, Mary took us fishing in the mornings. Well, my angels, you've almost got a keeper with that one, she'd say, even when we'd reel in a fish so puny and pathetic, we knew we'd have to throw it back.

Think so, I said. She's lovely.

Cheryl had light brown hair, thick and curly like Billy's; she had freckles, which, he insisted, formed the constellation Orion at the center of her nose.

She's the hardy, outdoor type, Billy said. Not another hothouse variety, like us.

That's good, I said. Besides, I like her. I'd met so many of Billy's friends, I couldn't tell whether or not he was serious. I never knew how friendly he wanted me to be.

She likes the dog, he said. She doesn't mind the music.

That's nice, I said. Shep got up from Billy's lap and stretched across mine; we usually avoided each other, but perched up in the loft together, we were forced to make accommodations.

Nice? Billy said. It's hell. I keep waiting for her to tell me all the things she doesn't like. The suspense is killing me. Sometimes I wake up in the middle of the night and just watch her, thinking any minute now she'll get up and tell me about everything I've done wrong. Living with someone who's agreeable can get pretty tricky.

Is he complaining about me again? Cheryl said. She climbed up the ladder, fed Shep a dog biscuit, passed a plate of cookies around for Billy and me. It's the one thing I can't stand about him.

There, I told you, Billy said. Go on, let's hear the rest.

Cheryl shrugged. That's it. Is he always this grumpy when he's sick?

Always, I said.

When Billy was born, he had allergies, later he developed asthma; he was sick and wheezy from the day he came home from the hospital. Naomi wasn't as worried as she would have been if Mary hadn't been there. Mary was a trained nurse, she knew how to take care of him. Hersh was embarrassed watching Billy when he'd have an attack—he'd have to leave the room. Sometimes Mary would be so upset for Billy, she'd get tears in her eyes. Then I'd cry too, and Billy, still short of breath, would try to comfort both of us.

I promise I won't get sick again, he'd say.

But it's not your fault, Mary would tell him.

Hersh and Naomi seemed to think otherwise. Naomi was sure he did it for attention. Hersh was convinced Billy didn't outgrow it so he'd have an excuse not to play baseball. Every time he'd get sick, Billy would get so mad at himself, he'd end up mad at everyone else, too.

Never, Billy said, raising himself up on his elbows, coughing between words. I am never grumpy when I'm sick. It's just that everyone around me gets intractable. He kept coughing and I could hear a hint of the wheeze that used to alarm Mary and me.

Easy, I said, the way Mary used to. Easy. It'll be all right.

Cheryl ran her hand over his forehead, she rubbed his back and waited for him to catch his breath.

I'll call the club and tell them you won't make it, she said.

Bossy women, he said. All my life I've been surrounded by them.

And a lucky thing, too, Cheryl said.

By the time Michael arrived, Billy was asleep; Cheryl was looking tired; and I was ready to leave. I had us out on the street in time to catch the cab he'd taken from the airport.

I'm sorry I didn't get a chance to talk to her, Michael said.

But why? I said. We've met so many of them.

Hersh had called Cheryl "another one of the skinny ones." He must hang around by the soup kitchens the way other men go to singles bars, Hersh said.

Because she's different, Michael said. I wanted to compare notes. See if she's having as much trouble breaking into this family as I am.

You're reading an awful lot into this, I said.

It's you, he said, who keeps skipping the best parts.

The log that promised rainbow colors delivered only one, but at least it burned evenly and we didn't have to get up to poke it. Billy took out his roach clip and offered me the last bit of the joint. The smoke burned my throat so I passed it back.

"But it isn't just nice," Billy said, "it's all the stability. Cheryl wants to move in with me. If we do that we might as well get married. I told her I'd think about it."

"And?"

"And I'm not sure. She drinks out of the milk carton and puts it back in the fridge. She hides the toothpaste in the cabinet when she's done and I can't find it. When she makes me feel good, I start to worry about what I'd do if she decided to move out. Sometimes in the mornings, I reach for her before I let my eyes open."

"I know what that's like," I said. "The only way around it is for you to move out first. That's what I did." I didn't think it was going to be funny before I said it, but now that we were comfortably stoned, it seemed hilarious.

"You're right," he said, "that's the only thing to do."

"Damn right," I said. "I'm hungry."

We scrounged around the kitchen; all we found was a pitcher of orange juice, a box of blueberry muffins, a lone pear with soft brown spots, and an apple.

"It's enough," I said. I sat down at the round glass table in the kitchen and used a small knife to work the soft brown spots out of the pear.

"Wait," Billy said. "I am about to perform the greatest miracle you may ever see in your life." He left the room and returned with a giant bag of M&M's. "Just promise you'll save me the greens."

I used to make him close his eyes and taste each color to see if he could tell the difference. When he kept guessing right, I'd blindfold him, turn out the lights, and still he'd know the green ones. Once I put a clothespin on his nose but he knew. Talent is talent, he'd say.

"I've got this theory," he said. He popped five green M&M's in his mouth, rolled the brown ones in my direction. "Food is more important than sex."

"Definitely," I said. "Besides, it's a lot easier to get a really good meal."

"I'm serious. I read this article that said if you started out hungry, then had sex, you'd still be hungry when you were done." He scratched his head and pulled at his moustache. "No, wait, that doesn't sound right."

I kept nodding and eating M&M's. "It's right. I know what you mean. Hunger stays with you."

"Is that it?" He mixed two yellows in with the greens and ate them from his palm.

"I've got this theory," I said, though it was only just forming, now that I was a little wrecked, "when someone's dying, all everyone talks about is food and sex, because . . ." I couldn't hold onto the thought. "Oh, God, Billy, I'm supposed to pick out her clothes tonight. I don't think I can do it."

"Don't," he said, "I'll help you tomorrow. We ought to just go to sleep."

But after an hour of trying to sleep, I called into Billy's room, "Do you think we'll know when it happens? Do you think we'll have some way to feel it without being told?"

"Every time I've had this sinking sensation and I've said to myself 'this is it,' I've been wrong. Right now I feel awful. I guess that means she'll make it through the night."

An hour later, I was still awake; I was sure Billy was too.

"What are you afraid of most?" I called to him.

"That she won't ever once say she loves me before she dies. Your turn."

"That she will."

10

"Aspirin, juice, coffee, please," I said as I walked into the kitchen in my old quilted-cotton bathrobe. The top four buttons had been missing for twenty-three years.

"Thought you'd say that." Billy, in his blue terry robe, playing maitre d', gestured for me to sit at the table. On a place mat he'd arranged a glass of juice, a cup of coffee, and two aspirins on a white plate. "Merry Christmas." He smiled and hummed "We Wish You a Merry Christmas."

"I know of perfectly sane women driven mad by men who were cheerful in the morning. There are stories about wives rolling over in bed and strangling their husbands. It's considered justifiable homicide."

"You need a second cup of coffee. Or should I just start a caffeine IV?" He was humming a medley and segued into "O Holy Night."

"Have you called the hospital?"

"I spoke to the nurse. Everything's the same as yesterday. I said we'd get there around eleven."

"To your health." I raised my cup, put it down, and lit a cigarette.

When the phone rang, we looked at each other and didn't move to get it. "I can't," I said.

"Neither can I." He picked up the receiver and handed it to me.

"Listen, children," Hersh said, "there's no reason for you to get here before ten o'clock. When you come, bring me socks and a clean shirt. I don't think anything will happen today, but the doctors haven't been in yet."

"Can she still talk? Can she sit up?"

"Of course I'm up. I've been up for hours."

"No," I said, "can Mother still talk?"

"We'll talk when you get here. See you around ten."

"Merry Christmas, Merry Christmas," Hannah sang at us as we met her outside Naomi's room.

"How is she?" Billy asked.

"She had a rough night, a lot of discomfort. She can have her pills any time she wants, but she holds out until she can't stand it anymore. She says she won't take them because they make her groggy. She is one tough customer."

"She is," Billy said.

"Won't be today," Hannah said. "Not yet."

"I don't know anymore if that's good or bad," I said. "Can't anyone do something so she won't be in pain?"

Hannah looked around, then leaned closer to us. "Some hospitals, you know, they start a special kind of drip, use a lot of morphine. Then the patient just slips away. But here they won't do that. Besides, she wouldn't let them, neither would your father. They want every minute." She took off her eyeglasses and wiped them with the tissue she kept tucked in her sleeve. "Go on in, Dr. Landau's with her. Maybe he can give you some answers. But I doubt he knows any more than I do."

Lawrence Landau stood by Naomi's bed talking to Hersh. It was hard to read his face. Hersh had the glazed expression that meant he couldn't understand what was being said.

Dr. Landau stopped talking and shook our hands. I was surprised to see he was nearly my height, much shorter than Billy. When I'd met him before, he'd seemed so imposing. But today, with his clothes wrinkled and mismatched and his hair sticking out from the bare spot on the back of his head, he looked different, human. Hersh and Naomi had always treated him like a god. They were sure he was the one who had kept her alive.

Two days after the mastectomy, I'd seen Naomi sitting up in bed. By the time Dr. Landau made his rounds, her face was made up.

This is, he told the group of medical students who trailed after him, my secret love. The most beautiful woman in my life. A class act.

When he insisted she get out of bed, she was up and dressed at nine o'clock. When he told her to exercise her right arm, she spent hours squeezing a pink rubber ball just to please him.

Before you go home, he instructed her, don't get into bed right away. Buy yourself a new dress.

So she had Hersh take her from the hospital to one of her dress shops.

The day she woke up to find clumps of her hair on the pillow, he came to the house.

It's nothing, he said. At least yours will grow back. Mine—he rubbed his widening bare spot—is gone forever. Now get out of bed and let me see that pitching arm.

When he said she ought to go out more, she went out at least once a day, staying in for lunch if she had plans for dinner, staying home at night if she'd met her friends for lunch.

I will not, she told me on the phone, let this get to me.

For the past two years, The Girls in Florida had invited her to visit, but she said she couldn't sit in the sun, she felt uncomfortable in a bathing suit. And after all, she really shouldn't be more than a phone call away from Dr. Landau, from Larry. It was hard to believe that all along he was the same short, tired man who stood by her bed this morning.

Naomi slept; her breathing seemed strained. Each time she moaned, Billy and I looked at each other.

"How much longer?" Billy finally asked.

"No one knows. Her heart and lungs are still strong."

"But she's in pain."

Dr. Landau turned away from us and walked into the hall. Billy and I went after him.

"Please," I said, "can't you tell us anything else?"

"I've explained this to your father, I'll try to explain it to you. She doesn't feel the pain, she's under too much sedation. It's harder on you than it is on her."

"Can't you do something?"

"In all honesty, I can't. Once she's in the hospital, all we can do is try to keep her comfortable and wait." He touched us both on the shoulder, then walked away.

"This is indecent," I said. "This is inhuman. I will not die in a hospital."

"Easy, Bether, easy. We've got a long day ahead of us. Let's go downstairs, maybe get a cup of coffee."

Hersh came out of the room talking as if he'd been in the middle of a conversation with us. "Ready?"

"Don't let him see you're strung out," Billy said.

"Just give me a minute," I said. "I want to see if she's up yet."

Naomi's eyes were open. They seemed vacant at first, then she focused on me.

"Oh," she said, "you're still here."

"But you missed your boyfriend," I said. I'd never dared to tease her before. It was an unspoken rule between us, my life was open to jokes, hers was not. How she let me know this was a mystery; everything about her was.

Michael was always telling me I ought to find out more. He didn't understand that I wouldn't ask, she wouldn't answer. The older I got, the longer I waited, the harder it was.

"Larry was in a few minutes ago and from the way he looked, people might think he spent the night here with you. The nurses are starting to talk."

"You know what I've always told you," she said, "if enough people are saying the same thing, there might be some truth in it."

"So, all this time you've been stringing Hersh along. Lining up your next conquest."

"At least someone in this family should have a little fun," she said. "A little romance."

"What the hell's the matter with you?" Hersh said. "You're in here talking to her when she's supposed to be resting?"

"Sorry," I said. Naomi squeezed my hand and shook her head.

"Let her alone," she said.

"You too," he said to her.

"Be a second wife," she told me. "They're the ones who

Michele Orwin

have it easy." For years she'd been saying that. Second wives, she'd say, get all the presents, take all the trips. If you've got to be a first wife, she'd say, don't do it for too long.

Hannah came in carrying two glucose bags. She removed the empty one from the stand. "Breakfast in bed," she said. "Just what the doctor ordered."

Behind Hannah's back, Naomi rolled her eyes and made a face.

"Merry Christmas," Billy greeted the coffee machine, "shame you have to work today."

Hersh shook his head. "There's a screw loose somewhere." They'd been saying that about Billy for years.

Billy brought the coffee to the table. Hersh continued talking only to me.

"When I go back upstairs I'm going to start calling everyone and tell them to wait until Tuesday." He emptied his pockets while he spoke, counted his coins, took out two dollar bills and handed them to Billy. "Get me some change," he told him. "Now, we'll need the clothes here, Beth. I spoke to the undertaker and he said she'll need a slip, undergarments, you know what I mean. She won't need stockings, but if you think she'd like to have them, bring them. And what should we do about the wig?"

I played with the plastic coffee stirrer, I rolled it into a ball, and then watched it uncurl on the table. "I have no idea. I'll do whatever you want."

"What kind of answer is that? Of course you'll do what I want. I'm asking for your opinion." He had a low flashpoint: a small gesture, a word in the wrong tone of voice, and suddenly he'd flare into anger.

"I'll bring the wig," I said.

"Do you know which one? She has two, but she only likes one of them."

"I'll bring both and you can tell me."

"Fine. Shoes. Or did I say that already? And jewelry, nothing good, maybe earrings."

He picked up his pipe to light it, put it down. He reached over and patted my hand. "I'm glad you're here," he looked right past me, "glad you're here. Who knew there'd be so much to do? I always relied on your mother to take care of these things. What do I know? Now when I need her, where is she? Did I tell you about the clothes?"

I nodded. "Don't worry," I said, "we'll help."

"Is there anything you want me to do?" Billy asked him.

Hersh shrugged. "What can you do?"

"Anything," Billy said.

"I seriously doubt that," Hersh told him.

Billy didn't answer. He got up from the table and walked away.

"Couldn't you try," I said, "to be a little easier on him?"

"I can't be worrying about the two of you now," Hersh said. He rubbed his eyes, his voice started to break. "What the hell difference does any of it make?" He took a drink of water and cleared his thoat. "I'm going back up. You suit yourself, no hurry, take your time."

Billy had left an unopened package of Oreos on the table. I knew if he was really upset he'd be back for them.

"If I ever let myself get mad at him," Billy said and sat down with me, "I'm afraid I'd never stop. I'm growing an ulcer with his name on it."

Hersh dozed, Naomi slept. Hannah took the newspaper from Hersh's lap and read it. She got up once to wash the newsprint from her hands, then settled down with the crossword puzzle. Billy and I were trading magazines we'd already read when three little women bustled into the room at one time. They kept knocking into each other, knocking each other against the doorframe. They wore coats and hats of curly gray fur that matched their hair. They wore their best shoes, carried handbags the same color. Their lipstick was too dark and their rouge too obvious. Their voices were so loud, even Hersh woke up. Three of our little aunts had come to visit. Cousin Milton drove them up from Bradley Beach and waited in the lobby while they scurried about the room hugging and kissing and clucking their tongues.

"*Oy*," they said, one right after the other, when they looked at Naomi. "*Gotenyu*," each one said in turn.

Aunt Rose took me by the hand and led me to the small vestibule.

"This," she said, "does not look so good. What's going to be with your father?"

"He's all right. He's been staying here."

"I know. I know. I call but I never get through. I want to tell him to come stay with us, but I never reach him. Essie says, 'Keep calling, keep calling.' 'What do you think I'm doing,' I tell her, 'checking the weather? But you know Hersh,' I say to her, 'remember the time with the television?' She says, 'Rose, who could forget such a thing? What are you, getting senile?' 'Like a fox,' I tell her, 'like a fox.'"

No one could forget the time with the television. We were having Hersh's family to dinner. There'd been unspoken arguments all week. Hersh had chosen a Sunday, Anna would be off, Naomi would have to hire a caterer. Hersh didn't want a caterer for his own family. Fine, Naomi had told him, then you fix dinner. What's wrong with cold cuts?

he wanted to know. That was just the kind of question Naomi loved.

You want to try it and find out? she said.

Since you put it that way, he said, yes, I do.

When the family arrived it looked like the circus; dozens of little aunts and uncles tumbling out of one car, two on each side of our grandparents.

The table, Aunt Rose pronounced, is lovely.

Cold food? Aunt Essie asked, loud enough for Naomi to hear her in the kithen. He invites us up here to give us cold food?

Aunt Bertha inspected the table. She picked up the platter of meat and brought it into the kitchen. Naomi, dear, this corned beef does not look lean to me. If I were you, I'd wrap it right up and take it back. Bertha picked up a piece of corned beef with her fingers and showed Naomi the white line of fat along its side.

If it were anyone else, Naomi would have agreed and thrown out the offending pieces of fatty meat, but this was Hersh's sister and whatever any of Hersh's sisters said was wrong.

Thank you, Bert, darling, but it'll be fine. You'll see. Now, if you'll just put the platter back on the table. She guided Aunt Bertha into the dining room.

Bertha shrugged at her sisters. Who can eat this? she asked them when she put the platter down.

There were so many people talking, no one noticed at first that Hersh wasn't with us. But once everyone's plates were filled with cold meat and fish and pickles and mustard and kaiser rolls and pickled tomatoes, and Aunt Rose said, You should have told me this was the kind of dinner you were having, I would have brought chopped liver—you know how Hersh loves my chopped liver—then we all realized Hersh wasn't even there.

William, darling, Naomi said in the tone of voice she saved for company, please see if you can find your father and tell him dinner is ready.

Hersh sat in front of the television with a roast beef sandwich in his hand. Arnold Palmer was one stroke behind. Did they really expect him to leave now?

Billy whispered to Naomi that Hersh was watching a golf match.

What kind of manners are these? Naomi said. You know I don't permit whispering at the table. Now where is your father?

Golf match, Billy said.

The sisters began talking to each other, translating into Yiddish for our grandparents. Naomi sat straight-backed and silent.

Hersh returned in time for coffee and no one said anything about where he'd been. Then the meal was over and everyone was at the door again, hugging and kissing and chattering. Hersh's mother put her hands on his ears and bent him toward her so she could kiss him on the forehead. You're a good boy, she said.

Nearly thirty years later, they still talked about it. The one time he invites us to the house, serves us cold food and then watches television.

This, Aunt Rose would say, is how she lets him treat his family. I had indigestion for a week from that meal. Bertha tried to tell her that the corned beef wasn't lean, but she didn't listen. To this day I can taste the greasy food in my stomach.

His sisters complained, but they still doted on him. They knew it wasn't his fault. They had taken care of him before Naomi had come along and they would be there to take care of him after Naomi had gone.

"You want to live with us," Bertha said to Hersh, "there's always room."

Essie, Bertha and Rose clustered one last time around the bed, then shook their heads and left the room. Hersh went with them into the hall. They told him to take care of himself. They made him bend down and each one kissed him on the forehead, leaving bright red lip prints above his eyebrows. They told him to call.

Then Aunt Rose hugged me.

"My poor baby," she said. "It's not easy to lose a mother. Especially for a girl."

I didn't know what to say to her. Except for Billy, everyone had been acting as if this would be Hersh's loss alone. We were all there to comfort and watch over him, it was what he expected. This was his show. At first it had been Naomi's, but by now everyone agreed it was a blessing that the end was near, so Naomi was blessed, and Hersh was suffering, and everyone else was to serve as audience and witness to his grief.

"You need anything," Rose said, "you call me. Understand?" She took my chin in her hand. I looked away. "Cry," she said, "what else can you do?"

"Come," Aunt Essie said, "it's time."

Aunt Bertha was holding Billy's hands. "Now," she said, "it's time you got a wife. You won't have your mother around to take care of you."

"I'm working on it," he said.

"Then I'll go buy a dress for the wedding." She pinched me on the cheek. "As long as no one's counting, I'll wear it to yours, too."

One morning last spring when I was resting my head against Michael's chest and his skin felt so smooth and warm I thought I could never grow tired of touching it, he said, Being married can't be that different from living together. It's just a piece of paper.

So is divorce, I said. So's a college diploma, a driver's license and a parking ticket.

Michael went wild whenever he got a parking ticket. He fought each one in person.

You're missing the point, he said. He sat up. I hated losing the warmth of his shoulders.

No, I'm not. Just my luck, I said, a first wife twice.

11

A young woman in old jeans and new sneakers occupied my usual chair in the lounge. She had the look of someone who's spent time waiting around hospitals—pale skin, circles under her eyes, restless. She closed her book over her index finger and smiled at me. Her face was familiar, but I couldn't place her.

"You're the one with the mother," she said, "I saw you last time you were here."

"Yes," I said, "I thought I'd seen you before. But after a while everyone starts to look . . ."

She waved a hand in front of her face to dismiss what I was saying; she was in a hurry to talk. "My father's dying too," she said. "Stomach cancer. He's on forty-eight-hour notice."

"I never heard that before."

"That means they're giving him only two days to live. So far they've been wrong." Her hands circled her face. She pulled at her hair. She played with one of the four earrings in her ear. "Your mother's on twenty-four-hour notice. I heard the nurses talking."

"I know," I said. My hands were out in front of me now and I noticed a ragged side to one of my thumbnails. I opened my pocketbook to get an emery board. I worked the one nail smooth, then carefully filed all the rest.

"I didn't mean to upset you," she said.

"Oh, no, you didn't. It's just that I'd never heard that expression before."

"I really thought you knew. Your father knows. He and my mother sit up in the lounge and talk at night. I'm glad she has company—she won't ever leave. Does your father go out?"

She was talking too fast and getting into my life too quickly. I needed to get up and walk around. When I sat down, I picked a chair closer to hers, but I still wanted my regular one back. "My name is Beth," I said.

"Joanne," she said. "My father's an old soul, you know. If he goes now, he might not come back. But your mother, she looks kind of new. You'll see her again."

"I'm glad," I said.

"You say that now," she said, "but who knows what she'll be? She could come back as one of those shoe salesmen who make you feel so embarrassed you end up buying shoes that don't fit. Expensive ones. She's got that kind of aura."

Well, Naomi did and she didn't, but I wasn't going to admit it to Joanne. It had to be a crazy guess, she had no way of knowing how many pairs of uncomfortable heels my mother had persuaded me into buying.

"I know you've got a brother here, and another one who's coming, and a sister. The brother who's here, he isn't married, is he?" Her eyes were so glassy she might have been speeding; her hands flew everywhere. She caught one hand with the other and tried to hold them on her lap.

"No, he's not. He'll be here in a minute." If he didn't come save me soon, I'd have to go find him. Billy had worked for a while in a drug-rehab clinic, he might know how to talk to her. "I'm sorry about your father. How long has he been in?"

"A week this time. A month last time. You know how it goes. But the shitty thing is, I haven't cried yet." She twisted her hair around her fingers. "I keep wanting to cry but I can't. My shrink says if you don't confront your grief now, it sneaks up on you later. It's like a time bomb waiting to go off. But I can't make myself cry. Can you? No, don't answer," she said. "You're probably the type who needs an old movie for an excuse. A book or something, before you can really let it out."

"I think I'd better see about Billy. I'll be back in a minute," I said. "You're going to be okay, aren't you?"

"Yeah," she said, "I'm okay. Does he live alone, or has he got a lover?"

"Be right back," I said. "You can ask him yourself."

Billy was in a phone booth by the elevators. He cracked open the door and motioned for me to stay.

"Don't know yet," I heard him say. "I don't think I should, but I'll let you know soon. . . . Thanks, I appreciate that. I know you do, Babe, I do too. . . . No question about it, it would help to have you here. But I've got more than I can handle as it is. I'll call later."

I thought about stepping into the phone booth next to

his to call Michael and tell him that yes, it really would help to have him here. But I'd promised myself I'd get through this alone. If I still wanted to, I'd call him when it was over.

"Cheryl," Billy said when he'd hung up the phone. "Why don't you go back to New York tonight?"

"I'm supposed to play at a party later." Billy worked in a library during the day, he only played piano for a few singers at night. "Ilene's booked us at a party in SoHo. But I've got a backup I can use."

"Go," I said, "you need a break."

"It doesn't feel right, first of all. And second of all, I won't go unless you come with me. You can stay over at my place and we'll catch a bus back in the morning."

I was working my way into a fine state of loneliness and I didn't want to be talked out of it. "I'd rather spend the night alone. Honest. It's getting kind of close around here anyway. Go. Please."

"Not without you."

"We'll talk about it later."

Joanne was waiting for us in the lounge. The smile she gave Billy was different from the one she'd given me.

"Another fan," I whispered.

"She's just a kid," he said.

As soon as we sat down, Joanne started talking eighty miles an hour; her hands were doing ninety. They jumped from her lap to Billy's. She kept moving closer, asking him questions, then not letting him answer. How old was he, and where did he live? What did he do, and did he believe in an afterlife or a past life and what was he before? Was he by any chance gay, or possibly bi, and did he have a lover, in this life or any other, and if he did, did it matter, because she had a guy, alive right now in Yonkers, but she wasn't always faithful, and was he busy tonight?

Billy calmed her by taking a long time to answer. He said, without ever saying so directly, that he was involved, but otherwise he would have been happy to go out with her. He took her hands and put them back on her knees.

"Did you ever ask yourself," she said, down-shifting, "if you could pick which one of your parents should die first, who you'd choose? Because if I could, I'd have chosen my mother. You know some places they believe that it's only with the mother's death that the children actually come to life. Now it's all screwed up, isn't it? They've got the wrong one in there. I'll probably have to come back ten times until they let me out of my contract."

"I'm really sorry," Billy said.

"Don't bother," Joanne said. "I don't need your pity. There are plenty of other people I could be with right now, interesting people. I feel more sorry for you. Both of you." She stopped talking to us and opened her book. We could see red half circles on the back of her hand where she'd dug her fingernails into the skin.

Everyone was so quiet we could hear the noises in the corridor, the sound of the trays being brought around. Somehow it was time again for another meal.

Billy and I checked our watches.

"I guess we're supposed to be hungry," he said.

"We could pretend we didn't notice," I said, and we both turned our chairs toward the window.

"Hey, you guys, I hope you haven't had lunch yet." Molly leaned over the back of Billy's chair and kissed him on the mouth. She messed his hair when she straightened up and blew me a kiss. "You didn't think they'd let Naomi in this place without me, did you?"

Molly was the one nurse Naomi liked, she'd been with her since the first operation. Something special had clicked with Molly and our parents and she became part of the circle of very close friends who were more like their family than we were.

She looked like a model and would have been one if she hadn't made the mistake of marrying too young, divorcing too soon, and needing a career that would give her time to take care of her son. Still, she was pretty enough to stand out among all the other nurses and she had the one quality Naomi admired in a woman.

You see, Naomi was always quick to remind me whenever Molly was around, she knows how to make the most of herself, Beth darling. That's something you really ought to learn.

And Molly was spunky. Naomi liked that too. Not like some people I know, Naomi said, who are afraid of their own shadow.

Whenever Naomi was in the hospital, Molly would take the late-afternoon or early-morning shift. When Naomi was home, Molly would stop in once a week to visit. She asked Naomi for advice and then followed it. Not, Naomi was quick to remind me, like some people I know.

Naomi joked with Molly and told her more about her life than she'd ever told any of us.

Your mom's really something, Molly always said. Molly and Hersh were the only ones who called Naomi "Mom."

"I thought I'd come in early since I was off yesterday," Molly said. "I wanted to see how your mom was doing. But I don't have to work yet. I'll leave my coat in the room and we'll go down for lunch. How is she?"

"She's been sleeping all day," Billy said.

"I'll have her up this afternoon." Molly met an intern in

the hall, linked her arm in his and went toward Naomi's room; she came back on the arm of another intern. "They're sleeping like babies," she said. "Let's go."

The cafeteria for doctors and nurses was one floor down from the coffee shop. Because the food was cheap, it was considered a privilege for outsiders to eat there. The public-relations office handed out passes only to family members of certain patients. Each time Naomi was admitted to the hospital, the first thing Hersh did was arrange for passes to the cafeteria so we could eat dinner in style.

Molly found us a table in the middle of the room and was giving us a rundown on everyone before we sat down. "Now you see that woman over there," she said, "the one with all that dark hair on her upper lip. I don't know why she doesn't do something about it, but anyway. She was having an affair with the radiologist over there," she pointed to a chubby man by the window, "but, and this is the good part, he was also fooling around with her best friend." She shifted in her seat and waved to a blond woman in one corner of the room. "Of course they found out about each other. Now they don't talk and he's seeing another nurse. Or two. And this woman over here, the tall blond one, well, she was having an affair with that woman over there, the stocky, dark one and they both have husbands on the staff, and . . ."

"Stop," I said. I was having enough trouble trying to eat the food. "I think I saw this on television once."

"I know. I swear if I could write, there'd be a book in it."

"What is it with you people?" Billy said. "You're worse than rabbits."

"When I went into nursing, I couldn't believe it either.

But if it's going on all the time, you start to take it for granted."

"Then you ought to come to the library to see how the rest of us live. Hold on a sec, there are red and green things floating around in my vanilla pudding."

"Colored raisins," she said. "They do that every Christmas. Kind of makes it festive for us. Oh, God, someone just walked in I don't ever want to see. Don't turn around."

Billy and I turned at the same time. All we saw was a man almost as old as our father and as bald as the only hospital roommate Naomi had whose head was shaved before the operation to remove a brain tumor.

"Him?" I said.

"Uhhuh." She kept her eyes lowered. "We had a very serious thing. Very serious. I'm still not over it. But he's being charged with insurance fraud. Said we couldn't see each other until the case was settled. His partner and his wife are the ones who turned him in."

"Okay," Billy said, "let me get this straight. Is it safe to assume that almost everyone in this room has slept with everyone else?"

"Not quite," she said, "but close."

"I don't understand," I said, "why here?" In my office the most we had was a rumor about Roz and Greg that surfaced every year at the office party and then died by mid-January.

"I think I've got it figured out," Molly said. Naomi always told me she thought Molly was savvy. Savvy and spunky. She had a line on everything. She could read people. Just like Naomi. "There are a couple of reasons. You see, you've got all these nurses who are so used to handling bodies all day, they're completely uninhibited. Then you're constantly thrown into life-and-death situations, which gets the adrenaline pumping. You've got all these spare rooms with empty beds. All the recreational drugs you could want. And besides, doctors are really good fucks."

"Are you sure about that?" I said. "Have you ever asked their wives?"

"No kidding," she said, "these guys study anatomy for years. I'm not saying they're any good emotionally, but technically they're very proficient."

"So," Billy said, smiling and tugging at his moustache, "you're telling me I'm surrounded here by hordes of uninhibited women?"

"Down, boy," she said, "I heard you've got someone at home."

Late in the afternoon, Hersh came into the lounge; he was starting to shuffle his feet the way the patients did. He looked out the window, talked to himself, and sat down. He tapped his pipe on the side of the ashtray to empty it, then filled it again. He lit a match, and while he worked at lighting his pipe, his eyes focused on us.

"Here you are," he said. "I've been looking all over. She's up, she's been asking for you. What the hell kind of thing is this? You're here to be with your mother and you spend all your time someplace else." He looked disgusted.

"We thought she was sleeping," I said. Billy touched my arm to signal I shouldn't try reasoning with him.

"How would you know what she's doing when you're in here?" He picked up his newspaper.

Molly sat alongside Naomi holding her hand and laughing. She wore a heavy, sculptured silver pin on her uniform. It was one of Naomi's favorite pieces of jewelry. I looked at it and looked away.

"Hey," Molly said, "look at this." She touched the pin. "It's my Christmas present. Isn't it beautiful?"

"It is," I said. I chewed at the raw spot in my bottom lip.

"Don't worry," Naomi said, "I've got one for you too. You'll see." She squeezed Molly's hand.

"Why don't you visit with your mom? I'll be right back," Molly said.

Billy and I stood on opposite sides of the bed; he held her hand, I ran my fingers up and down her arm. She felt warm and soft, more substantial than she looked.

"You have plans for tonight?" Naomi said.

"Shh," Billy told her, "don't try to talk."

She struggled to move farther up in the bed. "Can't I talk if I want to? Tell me if you're busy tonight, I want to know."

"Billy's got a party in New York and I'm really tired, so I thought I'd go back to the house and get to sleep early."

"Good," she said, "that's what I wanted to hear."

"Can I get you something, do you need anything?" Billy said.

"A new lease," she said, "this one's running out."

"Shh," Billy said. There were tears in his eyes. Hersh had told us not to cry in the room, he said it would upset Naomi. Billy kissed the tips of her fingers. "I'll be right back," he said. "Don't go away."

"Me?" she said. "Never."

David Werfel, heir apparent to the seat of chief urologist, poked his head in the room. David Werfel was Dr. Arthur Werfel's son. "A doctor *ben* doctor," Aunt Rose would have called him, "a blueblood." Arthur and Ethel Werfel were friends of the family; David and I had grown up together. He used to be fat, with pockmarked skin. Jogging and a full beard had changed him into a handsome man. He used to be married and living in Connecticut. Now he was divorced and working in Newark. He stopped in to see Naomi the last time she was in the hospital.

He's always been such a sweet boy, she'd said then. I think he's always had his eye on you, she'd decided. From there it was just a small jump in imagination to have us married.

David was sweet but not my type, I told her. He was like a brother, and I already had enough brothers. I wasn't interested, I was in love with Michael.

It didn't matter to Naomi. Being in love with Michael and being married to a doctor were two entirely different things. The way I was dragging my heels with Michael would take too long to suit her. David was clearly available and, she had convinced herself, desperately in love with me. He'd already told her he was lonely. He said he wanted a family. He didn't have to come right out and say my name for someone of her subtle, intuitive ability to know he was referring to me.

She'd kept David in her room with some excuse last time and waited for me to arrive. We talked, she watched, he suggested dinner, I was busy. I suggested lunch, he was working. Naomi answered for both of us, Maybe next time.

"Merry Christmas," David said. He kissed me hello, then bent to kiss Naomi.

"This," she said to me, "is my present. David, as it so happens, isn't busy tonight either. Isn't that nice, darling? You can have dinner together. My treat. But make sure your father eats first. Then you two can go out. For me," she said. "You wouldn't let a poor old woman down."

Either David had developed a charm he'd never had in high school or else he had beautiful bedside manners. "It'll be my pleasure," he said to Naomi. "My Christmas present, too. Well?" He looked over Naomi's head at me.

"Sure," I said. "Unless you really did have other plans."

"I'll pick you up around eight. I want to go home and shower first."

Billy and Molly were out in the hall.

"You can go to your party," I told Billy, "Naomi's made sure I've got company tonight."

David looked hurt. "I didn't mean it to sound that way," I said, "it's just that I feel a little awkward about this."

"If it helps, I would have asked you myself."

"It helps," I said, "it helps."

"Good," Molly said. I noticed the pin was hanging heavy on her uniform, making two small holes. "Now she'll get some sleep tonight."

In the few minutes we were away, Naomi seemed to have lost all her energy, she was almost asleep when we came to say goodnight.

"Make sure they go eat," she said to Molly.

"See what a good mother she is?" Molly's voice carried out of the room and down the hall. "She worries about you. I wish I had a mother like that. Go eat and make her happy. It's the least you can do. Right?" she asked Naomi.

"Right," Naomi said.

Hersh shuffled into the room. "Is she asleep? Does she know I'm coming back, I'm staying here tonight? That's the worst time for her. She doesn't like being alone at night."

"She knows," Molly said, "but she wants you to have dinner."

"Isn't she something?" Hersh said. "I've never met a more considerate woman in my life. Did I ever tell you how she's always been the one who's told me when to eat?

Everyone jokes that I'll starve without her. But it's true," he said.

For forty-five years, Naomi had told Hersh when to eat, what to eat, and most of the time she'd decided where to eat. He sat out every buffet line, while Naomi went through twice, once with a plate for him, later with a plate for herself. With her around, he never had to read a menu. She'd scan each menu for him and call out the food he liked. She told him when the vegetables needed more salt and when the chocolate mousse was too rich for him to finish. She selected the hard candies he carried around in the pockets of his coat. And when he went to the refrigerator in the middle of a television program, she knew what he ought to take for a snack.

"Well, what should I have?" Hersh asked as we went through the line in the staff cafeteria.

"There's not much choice," Billy said and Hersh started a slow burn. Neither of us knew how to tell him what to eat; we were used to living alone.

I tried. "Why don't you take some turkey and stuffing and sweet potatoes and green beans?"

"Beans?" He sounded insulted. "Me eat beans? I never eat beans. You know that. I don't know why I'm even asking the two of you."

"If I stay here one more minute," Billy said, "I'll start believing I'm mentally incompetent again. I think I need to get back home for a night."

"What is that, pumpkin pie?" Hersh said to the woman behind the counter. "I don't eat pumpkin pie. Don't you have apple? What about a brownie? Never mind, never mind," he said to her, though she didn't look at all interested as she stood with her soup ladle full of mashed potatoes. "I'll get something sweet at one of the machines."

Michele Orwin

He growled at having to pay the full five dollars since he wasn't having dessert, but the cashier wouldn't give in. Hersh shook his head. Except for a few doctors, and the private-duty nurses, the hospital was run by a bunch of morons. He saw it every day. Now they were offering him pumpkin pie and charging him full price and none of it would have happened if Naomi had been around.

12

Alone in the house, with two hours until David picked me up, I kicked off my shoes and left them in the front hall. I took off my coat and threw it over the back of the sofa. I couldn't shake the feeling that any minute Naomi would come down the stairs and remind me that my coat belonged in the closet, my shoes should stay on my feet. Especially in winter. How many times did she have to tell me going barefoot in winter was the best way to catch a cold?

The mail was stacked up on the counter in the breakfast nook. I looked through the pile of letters addressed to Naomi. Invitations to luncheons, private sales, fund-raising letters from the UJA, B'nai B'rith, Hadassah. A bill from the radiologist, another from the oncologist. A picture of the Venus de Milo and on the back an announcement of a sale at the Venus Boutique, one third off prosthetic devices and custom-made swimwear for "women who'd had surgery but still had style."

At some point, Hersh said, when he was reading from his list of what had to be done, we'll have to go back to the house and go through everything.

Do it when he's not around, Molly told us. Get rid of anything you can before Hersh goes home.

But what, I wanted to ask someone, do you do with it all? There was no one to ask. Tomorrow or the next day I'd call Roz; even if she didn't know, she'd have an opinion.

"And, Beth," Hersh said when I left the hospital, "don't forget the clothes."

We'd already forgotten. Billy offered to cancel his plans to help me. I told him I could manage if I drank my way through it.

But there wasn't one bottle of white wine in the house. I'd have to manage on hard liquor. I poured half a glass of vodka, lots of ice, a little water. I told myself what I'd been told, that it really didn't have any taste, and I went upstairs.

Naomi's walk-in closet was off to the side of her bed. I had to pass the two Styrofoam heads on her dresser. I raised my glass. Merry Christmas, ladies. I noticed that one of them was mostly gray. The style reminded me more of Mamie Eisenhower than of Naomi. My guess was she preferred the other, but I'd promised Hersh I'd bring him both.

I couldn't get beyond the hospital bed, the walker, and the bedpan without finishing my drink. I went downstairs for another. David would understand if I got a head start. He'd probably be happy to find me feeling relaxed. I returned to the bedroom ready to face the closet.

Billy and I used to sneak in there on rainy days to rub

our cheeks against her fur coats. She had one beaver jacket I pretended was our pet. Billy liked the awful little mink pelts with the heads and feet still attached. We never stayed long, the heavy smell of Chanel always made my nose stuffy.

The only story Naomi ever told us about herself was the one where she and Hersh met. They had both been invited to the same party. She'd borrowed her cousin's fur coat. If she looked rich, her mother told her, she'd meet a wealthy man. He'd borrowed his cousin's car. With a car, his sisters told him, he'd find a girl with money.

She thought he looked a little like William Powell; he was sure she was a dead ringer for Merle Oberon. He seemed like the kind of a guy who'd be the life of the party. She looked like the kind of girl to make heads turn. He loved the way she always smiled. She was taken with his sense of humor. They didn't confess they each came from poor families until after they were engaged.

Naomi wanted to call off the wedding, but her mother wouldn't let her. At twenty she was too old to be unmarried and living at home. Besides, did she want to be a secretary all her life? In America, her mother told her, sooner or later all husbands became rich. Hersh promised some day she could stop working and he'd be able to buy her everything she wanted.

He started his own business and she went to work for him. It took them ten years until she could quit her job, another five until they could afford their first house. Her dream was to have a lovely house, to decorate it with lovely children and to leave both the house and children in the care of well-paid help.

If I'd known then what I know now, she sometimes said, I'd have kept working. More often, though, she tried to press her dream on me. After all, she'd say, what kind of life would it have been without my family? There are advantages you can't always see. For their twenty-fifth anniversary, he bought her a fur coat of her own.

The furs were gone from the closet now; she'd put them in storage last year and hadn't been able to take them out this year. In their place were more clothes than I'd ever owned.

Naomi's ability to organize had always been a wonder to me; I didn't inherit a bit of it. Her casual dresses were lined up on the left, all in plastic bags, divided by season. Then her evening dresses, long and short. Next, blouses, winter and summer. At the far end of the closet was a small dressing table with a glass tray for perfume and a mirror framed in pink leaded glass. Along the right side were her slacks, her skirts, her jackets. Underneath them was a white velvet chair and the small step stool she needed to reach the shelves of shoes and handbags, scarves and sweaters, all stacked in clear plastic boxes.

I had to sit down. How could anyone get dressed in the morning when there were so many choices?

I checked my watch, I still had time for one more drink, and then I'd get this all taken care of quickly. Besides, after this one, David and I would glide through the small talk. He'd never suspect it was my first date in years.

I sorted through the clothes the way I would in a department store, hoping something would declare itself to be what I wanted. I imagined Naomi at my elbow saying, as she usually did, Beth, darling, don't be so difficult. Not every dress can be a drop-dead dress. Besides, you'll never know till you try it on.

Even with her swollen arms and legs, her stomach so distended she looked pregnant, I knew she'd want something simple but elegant, not too tight around the waist. There was a black knit outfit, full in the sleeves, elasticized waistband; black had always been her best color. But could you, did you, dress someone in black? Sharon would have known.

I placed the black outfit on the bed and went back to the closet. My plan was to select a few possibilities, then narrow them down to one.

I found the lavender silk dress she'd worn to Grim's third wedding. It was the last time I'd seen her dressed up. Would she want something with sentimental value if it had a small round stain on the cuff? Probably not.

Then I came across a rose-colored sweater and skirt she'd had made after the mastectomy but had never worn. It looked large enough, the neckline was flattering, the color was good for her; I put it down on Hersh's bed, my decision already made.

She would need shoes, but I never knew myself how to match shoes to a dress, a bag to shoes. Naomi would have found a way to get out of bed if she'd had any idea I'd be the one to be dressing her.

The trouble is, Beth, darling, she'd say after an endless day of shopping, you don't have enough confidence to have good taste. I'm sorry, I've done all I could.

I pulled down a dozen pairs of shoes all in their plastic boxes and considered each one carefully. Silver would be nice, but they were open in back, her feet would be cold. The black satin looked new, but the toes were closed and her feet might not fit. The black-and-silver then, but the heels were so high. Ever since she'd gotten sick, I'd tried to get her to stop wearing such high heels. Holding the shoes, I realized it didn't really matter if the heels were too high, she wouldn't be walking. I needed a refill.

I was starting to feel affectionate toward David. Naomi might be right, maybe we'd been interested in each other all along. It was more than coincidence that we'd both ended up single at the same time. And I could see now that Michael was all wrong. I should have realized it from the minute I saw that Cynthia person. Talk about lack of taste. Anyone who could have liked her could not have cared for me. No, that wasn't it. It was How could I have liked anyone who could have liked her? I knew I was on to something, I just couldn't think it straight through. I'd have to run it past Billy.

I balanced my glass on the foot of the bed and sat down to search through her dresser. Top drawer for lingerie. Tucked away in one corner were the pamphlets from the hospital. I'd been there the night the social worker gave them to her.

The nurse had just come by with last-minute instructions and medication; Naomi's operation was scheduled for seven the next morning. Then a woman came in smiling too much and carrying an armload of articles. She introduced herself to us and said right away she'd had a mastectomy. She knew what Naomi was going through. If Naomi wanted to talk, she was there. If Naomi wanted to listen, she would talk. If Naomi wanted to rest, she'd leave her something to read. It was nothing to be ashamed of, you could lead a normal life.

That's very sweet of you, Naomi said, but I'm not interested.

Well, that's normal too, the woman told her. I'll be back tomorrow.

I'll never know, Naomi said, what makes some people tick. Now why would she think I'd want to talk to a complete stranger?

Do you want to talk to me? I said. Visiting hours were almost over.

Not really, she said, calm as always. I just want it to be next week, that's all.

I don't understand.

It's what your father and I say to each other whenever we have to do something we don't want to do. We say we wish it was next week. Then it would be over. Sometimes I think we've wished our whole lives away like that.

You'll be fine, I said, I'll be here in the morning.

Next week, she said, I'll be fine.

I put back the pamphlets and scooped up a handful of silky things to pack in the bag. Someone else would have to make the selection.

There was still time to shower and slip into something nice of my own before David arrived. It must have been the vodka that was making me think how good it would feel to have someone just hold me for a while. I'd wear something suggestive enough to interest him, not sexy enough to scare him. But Hersh had told me to bring jewelry. I'd do the jewelry first.

Naomi always kept her jewelry in the middle drawer. Now, instead of the dark blue velvet cases for rings and earrings, she had four white boxes with our names on them. I took out the one labeled "Beth." Inside were all my report cards, my class pictures, my letters home from camp, my Red Cross junior lifesaving patches, my one honorable mention award for archery. A lifetime of Mother's Day cards and birthday cards and a stack of cards written out by some florist neither of us knew. I'd forgotten I'd ever made so many pictures and poems. She'd barely acknowledged most of them, and when she did she'd always seemed dissatisfied. There was the yellowed clipping of the announcement of my engagement to Jim, a dried corsage from a dance recital, beads from a baby bracelet, some baby teeth, a lock of hair tied with a pink satin ribbon, the postcard Michael and I had sent last summer from Nag's Head. A picture of me on Mary's lap.

I was about to look through the rest of the boxes when the doorbell rang. I shoved my box back with the others and shut the drawer.

With the stairs rolling away from me like an escalator, it took me a few minutes to get to the door. David rang five times, then started knocking on the window.

"Hi," I said. I could feel myself grinning hard the way I do when I'm stoned or drunk. "I've been trying to pick out clothes. And—" My tongue was too thick for me to talk. I needed to hold onto the door for support.

"That's all right," he said, "I'm early." He looked at me, still barefoot, my own clothes wrinkled from sitting around the hospital all day. "Why don't you finish getting dressed?" When he closed the door I almost fell.

"I wish I could, but I think I'm going to be sick."

"You can't do that," he said, "I'm not on call tonight."

He helped me into the bathroom, and he held his hand to my forehead. When I was done he wet a towel and washed my face with cold water.

"Some date," I said.

"I've had better," he said.

"Believe it or not," I said, "I've had worse." Then my knees gave out and he picked me up and carried me upstairs.

13

I woke up with the feeling I'd been undressed by someone else. It was more than the afterimage of one of those dreams where I find myself riding naked on the subway or I step out of the ocean and discover my bathing suit's gone. I couldn't remember how it happened, yet I had the very definite impression it had. Besides, there was proof—I wasn't wearing socks; and I always slept in socks. Even with Michael. More proof—my clothes were folded neatly on the chair by my desk. I was wearing a nightgown I hadn't worn since high school. I looked around for other evidence. There was a card propped up by my old teddy bear: "Don't worry, I still respect you. David."

Every time Naomi tried to fix me up it ended badly. Once we'd gone out to dinner and were seated next to friends of theirs I'd never met who had a son home from college. I thought the son looked smug and intolerant; Naomi thought he looked nice. Somehow, without my consent, a date was arranged. His parents would give him their car for the night; my parents would give him their daughter.

He was a wrestler at Rutgers with a walletful of false IDs I could use to be served liquor in New York, and what seemed like four more hands than I had. After I'd scooted back over to my side of the front seat for the tenth time, he turned the car around and brought me home. He was out of the driveway before I was in the door. Naomi, convinced I must have done something rude and embarrassing, swore she'd never try to help me again.

But, one day, during my first year in college, I got a call from a boy at a school nearby. His mother had met my mother, my mother had given his mother my phone number, his mother had promised he'd call. Would I want to go out? Sure, I said, why not? Well, because. He was pledging a fraternity, strictly WASP, they didn't know. He could ruin it if I were the wrong type. Did I look real Jewish or anything? Could he come over and meet me first? I'm sorry, I said, they should have given you a picture. I've got an awfully big nose. Give me your number and I'll let you know if I ever get it fixed.

So he wasn't perfect, Naomi said. Why must you make a federal case out of everything? He might have had friends.

I called David and left a message with his service that I'd be out all day. I picked up the clothes I'd chosen for Naomi along with the shoes and underwear, the two wigs, and I packed them in a small suitcase. Then I called the hospital and spoke to Hannah.

Again, Naomi had had a lot of discomfort during the

night. She'd only agreed to take her medication an hour ago. She was resting now. Hersh had just dozed off. Would I please bring *The New York Times*, and did I know where my mother's friends got those wonderful blueberry muffins, they might be nice today.

Naomi lay in bed with the white sheet tucked tight around her; the tubes made that gurgling noise I heard only when I first came into the room. Her skin was starting to look waxy. She looked smaller than she did yesterday, older. I needed to touch her to be sure she was still living. I ran my fingers over her hand.

Hersh slept in the green chair that doubled as a cot. Hannah sat by the window reading the Bible.

I gave Hannah the newspaper. "No muffins," I said.

"That's all right. Why don't you sit here so I can run down and get some coffee? She'll be asleep for a few hours more."

Hersh snorted, his head jerked from one side to the other, he licked his lips, and opened his eyes. He rubbed his hand over his face. "Well, well, well," he said in the distracted way he'd picked up the past few days. He rolled his neck to get the cricks out, then looked over at me. "Oh, it's you."

"Morning."

"She looks good, doesn't she?"

I nodded. I wasn't sure how many more days I could pretend for him.

"You know she woke up this morning and she looked at me and she said, 'Am I there yet?' She meant was she in heaven. I said, 'If you were, do you think I'd be sitting next to you?' Amazing, isn't it, what people think of?"

"It would be nice," I said.

"Nice isn't exactly the word I would use, but have it

your way." Whenever Hersh was upset, he'd haggle over words. Without Billy to warn me off, I let him bait me into a fight.

"Nice is exactly the word I would use," I said. "Why must you always be so difficult?"

"Darling, if anyone's being difficult, it's you."

"Well, I see Sleeping Beauty is awake." Hannah sent us back to our corners for the time being. "There's a good-looking man outside who says he's your son. Grim. 'Hope it's not like the Grim Reaper,' I told him. But he said 'No, nothing like that.'"

Grim walked into the room slowly. He was a big man with broad shoulders and a small roll of softening muscles starting to show above his waist. He'd been half a foot taller than Hersh since he was thirteen. Hersh told him even then he might have more height, but he'd soon have less hair. Grim now had a forehead as wide as his palm.

He carried himself carefully, afraid he might startle Naomi, more afraid that seeing her would be a shock to him. When he saw that she was still alive, he came as close to smiling as he ever did.

Charles Aaron Asher, first son in the Asher family, could walk at nine months. He could speak in whole sentences before every other baby ever born, but he never smiled. Not once.

Naomi was so upset she called in the pediatrician. The doctor checked him over completely: pinched his pudgy knees, chucked him under the chin, tickled his feet, talked like Donald Duck. No luck. He closed up his bag.

There's not one thing wrong with him that I can see, the doctor said. Some children are just born grim. They don't smile. It's not serious.

Anna picked him up and said, Well, Mr. Grim, I could have told them there wasn't anything the matter with you. All you need is a lot of women to love you and a good dinner. The name stuck.

It was because the doctor smelled of cigars, Grim said every time he had to sit through the telling of the story.

You were only eleven months old, you didn't know about cigars, Sharon said.

I did, he said. Somewhere in my tiny primal memory I knew cigars smelled like shit. It was not a good test.

Even so, Naomi said, you were a somber child.

I was bored.

How could you have been bored? You had all of us waiting on you hand and foot.

A regular prince, Sharon said.

A king among children, Billy said.

Then smile for us, I said, I've never seen you smile.

Grim would try but he couldn't get his lips open, the corners of his mouth barely turned up. I feel silly when I do this, he said, I've tried, but I can't.

Pretty grim, we agreed.

Michael could smile with his eyes the way Billy did. When he was happy his eyes would sparkle and turn a clear bright blue.

Grim kissed Naomi's forehead and held her hand. She woke up.

"I made it," he said.

"I waited for you," she told him.

I called Roz from the phone booth. Not to worry about work, she said, Walt wanted me to take as much time as I needed. Everyone at the office was asking about me. There were messages all over my desk; most of them were from Michael. He'd called once to leave a message, then checked in four more times to see if I'd gotten it. It might not be her place to say anything, but if she were me, she'd call him. Married people lived longer, it was a known fact.

David nearly collided with me as he came around the corner fast. He was wearing his whites, his stethoscope stuck out of his coat.

"Hey, sailor, how're you feeling today?" He took my hand and automatically felt for my pulse. "You hit some pretty rough weather last night."

"Thank you and I'm sorry."

"First night jitters. I understand."

"It wasn't that."

"Maybe now's not the time."

I hugged him. "When did you get to be so nice?"

"After the divorce," he said. "Walk with me, I was on my way to see your mother."

"If she sees us together, she'll start planning for the wedding."

"Whatever she thinks right now can't hurt her. Or you."

Tall Grim with his large hands and his long feet, his thinning light brown curls turned gray and his green eyes hidden by sunglasses, stood outside Naomi's door and kicked at the wall. "Goddamn fucking world," he said. "Can't anybody do anything?" He looked like he was ready to pick up David and shake him until he got an answer. "Can't you give her something? Can't you disconnect something?"

David shook his head. "I know what you're asking, but once she's in the hospital there's nothing we can do. If anyone were to try to speed things up, they'd be at risk. Who knows if a nurse would report it, or another doc, or if the family would change their minds? We can't do anything but keep her comfortable."

"Comfortable? You call that woman in there comfortable? Have you seen her?"

"Look, they have instructions there will be no heroic measures—no one will do anything extraordinary to keep her alive. But until her heart and her lungs stop functioning, all you can do is wait. Her doctors will be around later if you want to talk to them."

"What a goddamn, shitass, fucked-up world," was all Grim said. He shoved his hands in his pockets and kicked the wall till the toe of his shoe was scuffed and turned in. "Well," he said finally, "what do we do?"

"We talk, we sit, we eat." I was so accustomed to the hospital routine I didn't question it.

"For how long?"

"No one knows."

"Shit." He came at the wall with his fist.

"There's a machine downstairs that serves hot soup."

I remembered how Grim used to eat quarts of chicken-noodle soup. Anna would make it for him. She'd cook two chickens and roll out the noodles, twice a week. Naomi said they all bent over backward to try and make him happy. But it was no use, she said, he was such a funny kind of kid—sensitive and serious, worried about the world. A bookworm.

For a while he was fascinated by religion; as a child, she said, he absorbed persecution like a sponge. He worried about the atom bomb and gas chambers, the possible end of most of the world, the probable death of all the Jews. His life was in danger and he was too young to do anything about it.

One time Anna took Grim to her house for the weekend. He was Anna's favorite and she wanted to do something special for him for his birthday.

In Sunday School, Grim had heard that Germans put

Jews into ovens to kill them. At Anna's house, when he heard her speaking German to her family, he started to get nervous. Then Anna asked Grim to keep her company in the kitchen, the way he usually did, while she made him a chocolate cake. When she opened the oven he began to cry. She had to bring him home.

Naomi told us he was the same way about summer camp. He'd heard on the radio that people in Europe were put on trains to go to camp and they didn't return. Even though he'd seen the color slides of Camp Summer Bird in the Adirondacks, and met Uncle Art, the director, he wouldn't go. Naomi couldn't coax him into it. He was sure he'd never come back. Naomi and Hersh were relieved when he took astronomy and their life went back to normal. He settled on philosophy and made a career of asking questions that never could be answered, which, Naomi always said, was exactly what she would have predicted he would do.

Typical narcissistic personality disorder, Sharon said at Grim's third wedding. His children were the only members of the wedding party. He keeps hoping he'll marry himself.

Lonnie, Grim had told us, was his best student. She was fifteen years younger than he was. Southern, Methodist, nothing at all like Grim.

He seems like a nice enough guy to me, Michael said.

Male bonding, Sharon told him. It's what Grim does best.

He does? Billy said.

Don't be foolish, Naomi said. He's still the same sad little boy who's afraid to leave home.

The level of self-deception in this family is incredible, Sharon said.

Don't start, Hersh told her.

Because you know I'm right, Sharon said.

There are times, Billy said, seated between Sharon and me, when I think how nice it would be to have a brother.

Naomi sighed. I thought when you all grew up it would be easier.

I looked at Michael to see if he was catching any of this; he pretended to be lost in thought.

Grim's two ex-wives had helped prepare dinner, a few of his old girlfriends were busy clearing plates. His students took turns tending bar and serving coffee. Everyone there seemed like part of his family; we were the only guests.

"All right, all right. Here's the young people, now where's the party?" Oscar Mason met us on our way to the elevator.

Oscar was our parents' oldest and closest friend. Ever since his wife, Helen, had died two years ago he'd been dating women young enough to go out with his sons. Even before Helen died, he'd been known as a live wire and a natty dresser. He had his shirts and suits made for him in London. He ordered his shoes from Switzerland. He had the clean manicured hands of a dentist. He was the only one who visited every day he was in town.

He's waiting for me to die so he'll have someone to go drinking with, Naomi said. Just remember, she told Hersh, the young ones only want you for your money. What else would they do with an old goat like you?

Oscar clasped Grim on the shoulder. "Well, Professor, how's it going?" He leaned down and kissed me on the cheek, he trailed his hand down my back to my hip. "And you, you're no longer jailbait. Too bad you got a fella. How is she this morning?"

"The same," I said.

"Not good," said Grim.

"Nonsense," Oscar said. "She's going to be out of here

in time for New Year's Eve." Oscar had walked us back into the room.

"That's what I've been telling her myself," Hannah said. "She and Mr. Asher can go dancing."

"Two left feet," Naomi said.

"Listen to her," Hersh said, shaking his head in amazement, "she says she'd like something to eat. Honey, you can't."

Naomi fussed with the tubes in her mouth. "I said we can't go dancing because you've got two left feet." She fell back against the pillows.

Grim went over to her. "Don't excite yourself," he said. "You don't want to dance, don't dance."

Oscar snapped his fingers and paced the room. "Tell you what," he said to Naomi, "you can't come to the party, we'll bring the party to you. We've done it before. Remember the time we had my birthday party in the hospital after Helen's hysterectomy? I'll take care of everything. After all, how many New Year's Eves is it we've been together, thirty-five?"

"Thirty-seven," Hersh said. "I remember because that was the year I had my first Oldsmobile. Damnedest thing, isn't it, how I remember things? Ask me what I ate yesterday and I couldn't tell you. But thirty-seven years ago, it's as clear as a bell."

"I think I'd like that soup now," Grim said.

Oscar was up and ready to join us. "You know me," he said, "I want to be where the action is."

"So tell me," Oscar said when Grim sat down with his can of chicken soup, "how do you manage it? You've been married three times, how do you get used to a new woman?"

Grim put down his spoon and leaned back in his chair.

Grim the forlorn little boy became Grim the college professor. He touched his fingertips together. "A better question might be, how do you manage to stay with only one woman all your life?"

Oscar's face lit up. "You've got me there. You know me, even when Helen was still alive, I was no choirboy. But I came home to her every night. With your father, it's another story. Naomi's always taken care of him. He won't know what to do."

Grim stared at him. "I'm not worried," he said. "In spite of what everyone thinks, he's a man who knows how to take care of himself. In fact he's probably the only person he knows how to take care of. He won't suffer, he doesn't know how." He went back to his soup.

Oscar checked his thin gold watch. "Wish I could stay," he said. "It's been fun, kids. But I've got a plane to catch. Maybe some night we'll take him out, show him the ropes. You and me." He punched Grim on the arm. "I'll go say goodbye to your folks. Take care of yourselves." His kiss on my cheek was wet and sloppy.

Grim was on his second can of soup when Hersh sat down.

"I called two days ago," Hersh said. "You should have come then."

"I'm here now," Grim said.

"And your children? We don't hear a word from them. What kind of thing is that?"

Grim met his first wife while he was in the Peace Corps. Alicia was Guatemalan. Hersh and Naomi wouldn't speak to Grim even after his daughter was born. They didn't visit him until his second daughter was a year old.

I have nothing against them, Naomi said. They're lovely little girls. But for some reason, I can't seem to warm up to them. I've tried.

They would have tried harder when Grim moved out if he hadn't moved right in with Carol, an Irish Catholic from Marblehead.

The girl was pregnant, Naomi said. He did the right thing. He just should have done it slower, that's all.

Patrick was born before Grim and Carol could get married. After the wedding, Naomi said, then we'll send a present. But they never did.

Grim's children were all teenagers now. Hersh and Naomi didn't have a picture of any of them. Naomi sent them cards for their birthday, but never told Hersh. Hersh sent them checks for the holidays, but kept it a secret from Naomi. As a couple they swore to each other they wanted nothing to do with Grim and his craziness. But one word from him that they'd be welcome in his house and they'd give in—while all along Grim felt victimized and virtuous, sure he was the one who was waiting for some sign from them.

"I've told them their grandmother is sick," Grim said. "I've asked them to call. That's all I can do."

"You can do a damn sight better than that," Hersh said. "You've got no control over your own family."

"It's better than trying to have too much."

They glared at each other. "Maybe you two want to be alone," I said. Neither one looked at me.

About a year ago, Michael had a meeting in Boston; he wanted me to go. If I could get a day off from work, we'd make a long weekend of it; walk around Cambridge, see Faneuil Hall, fill up on seafood, visit Grim.

Though Michael never said so directly, it wasn't his style, he had stepped up his campaign to make me come to terms with my family.

Life is not, I told him on the plane, one big group therapy session.

Exactly, he said. It's just a bunch of people doing the best they can. He took my hand and held it tightly. He liked to think he held onto me during takeoffs and landings so I would feel safe, but I wasn't the one who was nervous about flying.

Lonnie met us at the airport, dropped Michael at his meeting downtown, then took me out to school to sit in on one of Grim's classes.

He's the most exciting professor I've ever seen, Lonnie said. I chalked it up to the infatuation of a girlfriend and the adoration of a former student. My quiet, somber brother had never said an interesting word to any of us.

I settled back in the hard wooden seat and waited to be bored; but I never was. The man in the front of the long lecture hall, walking back and forth across the stage, pausing in front of the lectern only for effect because he didn't use notes, was, in fact, the most exciting professor I'd ever seen. Not one student fell asleep, not one minute of the class was wasted.

So many students gathered around him afterward, it took another hour until we were out of the lecture hall. And then there he was, sitting at lunch, my quiet, serious brother; Lonnie was the one who did all the talking.

Charlie, she said, you were good today, really good.

Charlie? I said.

Grim nearly smiled. After all, he said, it is my name.

When Billy and I grew tired of puzzling out Sharon, we'd try, sometimes, to get a handle on Grim. We argued about which one of us had had a harder time with him. Grim was the house hero, star student and athlete. When Billy turned out to have musical talent, Mary used to tell him to be proud of himself; she told him not to hide his light under a bushel. But growing up in Grim's shadow was too hard; Mary was the only one who noticed Billy had any light. I insisted I was even more invisible.

I was thinking about the time Grim brought home three of his friends. I was in the den reading.

Hey, who's the girl? they said.

Which one? Grim said.

The one with the long dark hair.

I don't know, Grim said. And it always seemed like he really didn't.

Hey, they said, she's right in there.

In that case, Grim said, she must be one of my sisters. If she's old and mean, she's Sharon, if not, it's the other one.

That's right, it is your name, I said to Grim across the table. I guess sometimes I just forget.

Lonnie laughed. She said they had the same problem in her family. She had so many brothers and sisters and each one had two or three nicknames and other names they liked to be called, she wasn't sure she could say for certain the Christian names of everyone in her family, either.

She was glad when Michael finally joined us and we could all go back to the house so she could get started on dinner. They had tried to get Grim's kids to come over but it didn't work out; so they were having some students and some other faculty members instead. And she had two of his papers to type.

But back at the house, Grim was the one to do his disappearing act, we didn't see him until dinner. And then, once again, he was transformed into the man I'd seen in the lecture hall. He acted as if we'd been friendly for years.

Only Sharon would have known what to make of it.

He's a great guy, Michael said. I don't know why you're all so funny about him.

At the moment, I said, neither do I.

We left with hugs and kisses and promises to keep in touch. Grim took out his calendar and showed me the weekends he'd circled when he thought they'd be able to come visit. He circled other weekends he thought would be good for us to come up there so he could go skiing with Michael. I didn't hear from Grim again until the night Hersh called to say Naomi was dying.

Hannah was gathering up her things and putting them into a Bamberger's shopping bag. She pulled off her white shoes and put on her short rust-colored boots. Then she wrapped a scarf around her neck and draped another one around her coat collar. "Presents from my granddaughter," she said. "Every year for Christmas, she makes me a scarf."

She put *The New York Times* in her shopping bag and took one of the new flower arrangements off the window ledge. "Your mother said I could have this one. Hope no one minds. They die so quickly in this dry air, it seems a shame."

"Go ahead," I said.

"Not tonight," Hannah said. "I can tell you that much. The rest is in the Lord's hands. But you keep her company, that's what she needs. Let her know she's not alone, she hates it so to be alone. I think that's why your father's sleeping here. She says she doesn't want him, but he knows she does. You stay with her till that young nurse gets here, I've got to go."

I stood by the side of Naomi's bed and held her hand. With my other hand I stroked her face, ran my fingers down her shoulder, over her arm. I imagined a quiet current flowing back and forth between us. For a moment it seemed that I was trying to give her my will to keep going, while she was trying to give me her strength to let go.

Billy must have been in the room a few minutes before I sensed him standing behind me.

"I didn't want to disturb you," he said. "Are you okay?"

"Fine. It's been a long day. Have you seen Grim?"

"He's outside with Molly. He says he's going back to Boston tonight. He's waiting to say goodbye."

"To me?"

"To Naomi."

"So," Grim said, "I'm going back." He hung his head and kicked at a loose piece of molding where the wall met the floor. "You two have things covered pretty much. If you need me I can be here in a couple of hours. But I won't be part of a deathwatch." He picked up the brown canvas suitcase.

"Wait," I said, "you've got the wrong bag."

"What?"

"That's the suitcase with Naomi's clothes. Yours must still be in the room."

"Oh, Christ, I can't go back in there."

"It's all right," Molly said, "some people can handle it, some people can't. At least you were here to see her. She wanted that."

Grim looked to Hersh for agreement.

"It's a fine how-do-you-do," Hersh said, "when your own children can't even take a day or two out of their lives to be with you at the end."

"Then I'll stay."

"No, go," Hersh said, "I don't want you here anyway.

If you can live with yourself, who am I to tell you what to do?"

"She's my mother, goddamn you. How dare you play your nasty little games with me now. What is so fucking wonderful about standing around here watching her die?"

I expected Hersh to tell him what he'd told us over and over, how he'd been in the room with his mother when she took her last breath. One soft little sigh. So easy finally, so peaceful. He wanted us to have that, whether we wanted it or not.

"You'll never know," Hersh said. "Seems to me walking out on people is your strong suit." Slowly he pulled his pipe from his pocket, bit down on it, then removed it from his mouth. "You children will excuse me, I'm going inside to be with your mother."

"If I don't go," Grim said, "I'm afraid I might kill him."

Billy and I walked with Grim to the front desk, where he called a cab.

"Nothing will ever change," he said as we stood at the curb. "How can you stay?"

Billy shrugged. "How can we leave?"

"I'll be in touch," he said and bent to get into the taxi.

I hate saying goodbye, I said to Michael as I stood at the door of his apartment. I'd managed to pack everything I kept there in one suitcase and one cardboard box.

I hate it, I said, but I always feel like I have to do it.

He didn't say anything. I'd played it out both ways in my mind. He'd ask me to reconsider and I'd refuse. He'd ask and I'd give in. Either way, he was supposed to say something.

Look, don't say anything, I said to him. It's taken me a whole year to work up to this. It's got to be right.

It probably is, he said.

Good, I said. Then we shouldn't go back on it.

I was saying everything the way I'd thought I would, I was acting as strong as I'd meant to show I could be. I could have carried it off if he hadn't checked the clock behind my head the way he did when he was hoping to catch the beginning of the football game, if he hadn't looked at me and stroked my cheek.

I really do hope, he said, you find whatever it is you want.

You too, I said. At least I didn't cry till I got all the way out to the car.

14

In the middle of the night, my legs felt so cold they ached. The tip of my nose, the tops of my fingers were like ice. I thought I heard Billy moving around in his room.

"Are you up?" I called to him.

"Jesus, I'm freezing," he said.

"Do you think?"

"My first thought."

"You call."

We sat next to each other, shivering, an old afghan over our shoulders, while Billy dialed the main desk. The nurse on duty said Naomi's condition hadn't changed.

"Then what do you make of it?" I said.

"Must be the pilot light on the furnace went out. Help me find a match and I'll fix it."

"Are you sure that's all?"

"Well, it could also be they forgot to order enough oil."

We both slept late and were slow getting started. We stopped at a diner for scrambled eggs and toast, and we didn't get to the hospital till afternoon.

Hannah, her arms folded across her starched white chest, guarded the entrance to Naomi's room. "Soon," she said, her voice low, "very soon now, I'm afraid."

I started to go inside but she shook her head. I could see the curtain pulled in a semicircle around the bed. There were five or six interns in the room. One was taking blood, another was checking Naomi's heartbeat, a third was monitoring her temperature and blood pressure. Hersh stood to one side.

"Awful," he said, "just awful. Why can't they leave her alone?"

"You know it's the rules," Hannah said. "They can't keep someone in the hospital unless they continue to run tests."

"All I wanted for her," he said, "was death with a little dignity. I wanted her to die like a lady. I can't stand it when they poke at her like this."

"Come," I said. I took his arm. "We'll sit in the lounge."

He leaned on me as he shuffled down the hall. At the elevator we saw Joanne and her mother, their coats on, waiting to leave. Two men, most likely her brothers, carried bags and boxes and flowers.

"He died," Joanne said. "We're finally taking her home."

Her mother clutched Hersh's hand. "The hard part's just beginning for us," she said to him.

"I know," he said, "I know."

Joanne grabbed Billy's hand and wouldn't let go until he'd stepped onto the elevator with her.

Hersh, in a daze, had turned himself around. He started heading down the hall the way we'd come. I caught his elbow and steered him in the other direction.

"Everyone's dying," he said. "You talk on the phone to your friends and if it isn't one thing it's another. This one's got trouble with kidneys, another one's got prostate cancer. We used to talk about golf, the stock market. Now all the talk is doctors and tests. Like flies," he said. "They're dropping like flies." He sat down.

"Now they're saying this is it. But they've been wrong so many times, it's hard to believe them."

"Maybe," I started to say, but he was reading his list, not listening to me. He put the list back in his pocket.

"I don't know what happened," he said. "She was up in the middle of the night, she was talking to me. She sounded so lucid. 'Make sure,' she told me, 'the grandchildren take something of mine that they want.' I said, 'In the middle of the night you want to talk about this?' "

Billy came into the lounge and pulled up a chair.

" 'What do I care what time it is?' she said. Just like that she said it—testy. You know how I've always told her she couldn't be so sick if she could still get mad at me. She was so angry, I thought she must be getting better."

Billy started to say something. Hersh held up his hand. "Let me finish. Then she says to me, 'The girls will be fine, I'm not worried about them. Grim too, he's got more women than he knows what to do with. They'll take care of him. But Billy, my baby, keep an eye on him. Make sure he's all right.' 'What are you talking about?' I said to her. 'William's a grown man.' 'For once will you listen to me?' she said. 'He's too good-natured, people will take advantage of him. You keep an eye out, make sure it doesn't happen.' "

Without saying a word, Billy got up and left the lounge.

" 'Any other instructions that can't wait till morning?' I said to her. Then," Hersh said, "she was out like a light, and she hasn't woken up since. I don't understand it. I'm telling you she was talking to me normal as could be."

Hersh stared out the window. I kept a book open in front of me, but I couldn't read it. People I didn't know wandered into the lounge but I didn't try to talk to them and they knew to leave us alone.

Billy came back an hour later. He motioned for me to move out of Hersh's hearing range.

"No problem," he said. There was a tear trapped in the short hairs of his moustache. "I took care of everything. I told her she doesn't have to worry about me anymore. Cheryl and I are going to get married. We decided a couple of days ago, I was just waiting for the right time to tell everyone."

"Hey," I said, "I'm happy for you." I kissed his cheek.

"She is too. I think. She didn't say anything, but I swear to God, Beth, it looked like she smiled." He took a small Milky Way out of his pocket, unwrapped it and ate it. "Anyway, don't mention anything to Hersh. I'm going back now to get Cheryl and we'll be out tomorrow to tell them together."

"Are you sure?"

He unwrapped another Milky Way. "No," he said. "But I'm beginning to think I'll never be sure. And Cheryl's as bad as I am, she just wants the decision made. Then we'll figure out how to live with it."

"Tell Cheryl she's lucky." I wiped a crumb of chocolate off his upper lip.

"I hate to leave you alone with him again," he said.

"He's not so bad," I said, looking over at Hersh. He slept with his head back, his mouth open. I could see the loose wrinkled skin around his neck, the lines that would never disappear from his face. He was starting to look old. He was starting to look like he wouldn't be around forever either. "He means well."

Hannah's shopping bag was full of magazines and candy when she stopped in the lounge. "I'll say a prayer for her and for the rest of you." She handed Hersh a bill. "You can give me a check now, then file with your insurance later. Some of these companies pick up most of it."

"I'll straighten this out with you tomorrow," Hersh said.

"If you'd prefer, Mr. Asher. Only I'm not sure you'll be needing me here tomorrow, but I'll still be needing my pay."

"Tomorrow," Hersh said, subject closed. He left the lounge.

"Your dad," Molly said, sitting down next to me, "is in one of those dark moods. It's better if I leave him alone. He's fighting it. I don't want to be around when he loses."

"I think I need to know now," I said, "what happens when somebody dies."

"It's not as bad as you think it'll be," she said, "After watching them struggle for so long, you almost feel happy that they've finally found peace."

"But what do you do?" I said. "Do you say a prayer? Do you make some kind of sign? If I'm the only one in the room then, what should I do?"

"One time I asked a rabbi that question. He said pray if you like, any prayer that comes to mind. And some people believe you should open a window to let the soul go free. So what I do first is open a window. It may just be a superstition, but at least I feel like I've done something."

I nibbled at a cuticle, I chewed my lower lip. The only prayers I could think of were the ones Mary taught me.

"You're afraid, aren't you?" she said.

I nodded.

"Then come on, let's go to her room. The more time you spend there, the less frightening it'll be."

The light over Naomi's bed was on, the rest of the room was dark. Hersh had been sleeping in the chair by the bed. He woke, said a few words to himself, stretched his legs, then announced he was going out to smoke his pipe, and left the room. Molly and I couldn't tell if he knew we were there.

Naomi moved around in her sleep. She seemed to be swimming under water, gasping for air. I listened to the small, pained noises she made.

"Don't worry," Molly said, "she can't feel anything anymore. The medicine must be wearing off though. I'm going to let it go a few more minutes so you can spend some time with her. She might still come around."

In the window, I could see our reflection, then dark clouds. We still hadn't figured out what we'd do if it snowed.

I did what I'd done a hundred times, I reached for her hand and held it between my own. It still felt warm. I stroked her face. I tried to remember what she had looked like before she was sick, but it was so dark and so quiet, I couldn't think of anything but listening for the sound of her breathing, the sound of my own measured breath.

She twisted slightly, then she opened her eyelids. Her eyes were filmy; that look of fear was gone from them, but I didn't know if she could see me.

"Shhh," I said, "it's all right, I'm here."

"My beautiful girl," she said.

"It's me, Beth," I told her.

"I always wanted," she struggled with each word, "for you to feel it inside, but you never did."

"I'm sorry," I said, "I don't understand." She didn't answer. I stayed by her bed and waited for her to wake up again. When I couldn't look directly at her, I watched her reflection in the window.

"I'm going to have to give her the medicine now," Molly said. I didn't know how long I'd been standing there. "Did she talk to you?"

"She did," I said, "but I'm not sure she knew it was me."

"Go home," Molly said, "get some rest. You'll need it."

I called Michael. I said I wouldn't, but I was in my parents' house alone, and after two drinks it sounded like the only good idea I'd had in months.

"Do you want me to come up?"

"Please," I said. "I need you more than I thought."

"Then I'll be there in the morning."

"I know she'll be happy to see you," I said.

"I'm not doing it for her," he said. "If that's your only reason, tell me now."

"You know me better than that," I said.

His promise to come and a third drink put me to sleep.

His plane came in at nine o'clock. I'd been at the airport since eight. "Thank you," I said when he came down the ramp. I felt a little shy with him. I needed time to get used to him again.

"You look awful," he said, but his eyes turned that clear bright blue, and he held me so long I was tempted to take him back to the house instead of the hospital.

"It's been rough," he said in the car. "If we get back together, it can't be temporary."

"I'll try," I said. "I promise I will, but right now nothing seems permanent."

I gave Michael a tour of the hospital. I wanted to fill the awkward silence between us. "This is the coffee shop where I've had two thousand cups of coffee. This is the gift shop where they won't give you change for a dollar unless you buy a roll of Life Savers. Here's the elevator." We got on for the short, silent ride up to the fourth floor. "This is the visitors' lounge where we fight and breathe smoke at each other," I continued. "Oh, and the water fountain, the service elevators. The woman coming down the hall is Mrs. Leonard, the man in the gray bathrobe is Mr. Grafman." I was trying to stall, do anything I could to delay starting another day of waiting.

"This is the nurses' station, in the back is the nurses' lounge. We've got some orange juice in the refrigerator there if you'd like. Some butter cookies, too."

He said he was fine, he rubbed his hands up and down my arms to warm them. "Fine, but chilly," he said. There was a draft somewhere.

"Funny," I said, "It's usually stifling. Here's Frosty the Junky." I showed him the snowman on the desk. "Here's where they lock up all the medicine. And here, at last," I said, "is my mother's room."

The first thing I noticed was the open window.

Epilogue

Even though it was one of those rare December days when the temperature shot from thirty degrees before breakfast to sixty-five degrees by lunch, The Girls all wore their fur coats. Since most of them had been in Florida and so had missed the funeral, they agreed they couldn't possibly miss the unveiling, too. And, they agreed, Naomi would have expected to see each of them in their deep, dark furs. They wore their coats out of respect.

The sun was melting the ice cover on the ground, turning the cemetery lawn soft, and as The Girls stood together in a circle, they kept switching positions to pull their sharp, high heels from the mud. With this year's relocation to Boca Raton and Miami Beach still a week away, their faces were pale and lined, making them look older, I was sure, than Naomi would have looked.

Grim's new baby, Nate, was the only other person wearing a jacket—a puffy blue jacket with a matching crocheted hat and mittens. Grim held him close to his chest in a canvas sling. The baby rested with his face turned to the side so everyone could get a good look. But Sharon refused to look at her new nephew.

"How could you think," she said to Grim right after he and Lonnie had pulled up and waited in the car for Nate to finish nursing, "that this is in any way an appropriate place to bring a baby?"

Grim shrugged and rubbed Nate's nearly round head. He stepped in front of Sharon to help Lonnie and the baby out of the car. He eased Nate into the sling across his wide chest. In the past year, Grim had filled out. His neck had thickened, his midriff was bowed.

If we could get a hundred dollars, Billy said the last time we all saw each other, for every pound this family's put on or taken off this year, we'd be wealthy people, Bether. We'd be goddamn rich.

Billy'd gone up fifteen pounds, I'd finally gotten down five, though one or two of those kept creeping back. Hersh had leveled off a little heavier than he'd been before Naomi got sick, and now he often wore jackets that couldn't close, pants that barely buttoned. Without Naomi, he said, he couldn't go shopping, couldn't get to the tailor; it was a constant struggle for him to adjust to his clothes. Grim was fat and as happy as he'd ever been; he swore he was getting laugh lines. Lonnie ate her way though her pregnancy and Grim, determined to be more supportive, ate with her. He'd spent his sabbatical learning to cook French Provincial dishes; he'd studied the art of using a food processor; he'd researched the subtleties of working a wok. And Sharon had grown so thin it was almost alarming. She now appeared both fragile and tough, older and younger—all bones and angles. Whenever I saw her she complained of being cold; her fingers were like icicles. The Girls couldn't get over how wonderful she looked.

"I, for one," Michael said, "do not think it's very attractive." He'd caught me as I was about to slip into a slight decline comparing myself to Sharon. Each time I saw her, I wished away a thousand dollars' worth of weight. "My guess is that she's probably sick," he said. "But you're all complimenting her as if she's done something wonderful."

He was still logical and reasonable. Nearly a year of fighting over apartments and wedding dates hadn't changed him. Probably nothing would, and I was going to marry him anyway. The future looked shaky.

With you, he said, it always does.

But you've got to admit I'm getting better, I said. And I believed I was.

We'd bought an apartment, though it had taken him months to convince me I wasn't signing away the rest of my life.

We can sell it. People do that all the time. Here, he said and sat next to me with the newspaper across our laps the way Hersh used to when I was little and he'd read me the funnies. Here, Michael said, opening to the real estate section: "Condominiums for sale." Every day of the week. We need it for taxes. If you'd bought your own place sooner, you wouldn't take it so hard.

Once he'd convinced me, I was the one who insisted we settle and move in before the wedding. If it didn't work out, all we'd have to do was put an ad in the paper; he'd promised me it would be that easy.

Then we bought a sofa. This is the part I hate about marriage, I said, you need all this stuff.

So far, he said, the sofa is man's best invention for letting two people sit next to each other in the living room.

The trouble is, I said, once you get something like this into an apartment, you never get it out. We'll grow old on this sofa. Our grandchildren will spill milk on it. We'll get incontinent on it. It'll go to Goodwill fifty years from now and get infested with silverfish.

I love you, Michael said, starting his new game, because you're such a romantic. Because . . .

Okay, you win, we'll buy it. Only if we ever get divorced, you've got to promise me you'll keep it.

But it was comfortable and durable and large enough for Michael and me to lie down on together and stare at the ceiling while we argued about our future and measured how miraculously well our bodies fit, shoulder to waist, hip to toe. After a while I even liked it.

And we'd decided to get married New Year's Eve. That way, I said, we'll know we've got something to do.

The cemetery was less frightening than it had been a year ago. Then it was terrifying because it had been so ordinary. Row after row of stone markers. Three other funerals within view with the same line of black cars, the same cluster of sad faces. And near where we stood, a rectangular hole in the ground, a large wooden box, flowers and chairs. It didn't seem to have anything to do with Naomi. A box, a hole, flowers. If Naomi had really been there, I was sure I would have sensed it, but all I felt was dizzy and queasy.

If I have to watch them actually put the casket in the ground, I whispered to Michael, I'm afraid I'll be sick. I was holding him so tightly I left marks on his arm.

Billy was popping Rolaids; Sharon was checking her

watch. The service was starting twenty minutes late and the funeral home had sent the wrong flowers. Grim was chewing fingernails he hadn't chewed in forty years. And Hersh was still fuming about the way they'd made Naomi look. When we'd viewed her, he was furious about how they'd painted her face and fixed her hair; her body, dressed in an outfit he hadn't seen her wear, seemed the wrong shape. He'd had to say goodbye to a woman he'd never seen before. Once again, in spite of everything he'd done to make things right, everything was going wrong. He kept expecting Naomi to give him hell for it.

It was so cold then, no one could stand still. The wind was so sharp it brought tears to my eyes. Bad enough that the rabbi had been late; then we had to wait for the aunts to arrive. It was Rose's fault, they all said as they rushed around hugging everyone and apologizing.

Aunt Rose wore a brown print scarf on her head, tied at her chin. She looked, Naomi would have said, like she just stepped off the boat. Afraid of making more of a fuss, she quietly squeezed in next to me.

I wanted to look nice for Hersh, she whispered, so I had Essie put in a rinse. Now look, she said and peeled back the scarf to show me hair the color of an orange. It made me laugh so, I nearly forgot what we were there for; I eased my grip on Michael's arm. The service was less wrenching than I'd expected, and we were gone before they lowered the box into the ground.

But there was no one to make me laugh four months later when we gathered at the same cemetery around Aunt Rose's grave. Liver cancer that took her so quickly everyone said if you had to go, it was better to go that way. Leave it to Rose, they said, to speed things up. She didn't even have time to start chemotherapy or radiation. But that was for the best, Aunt Essie said and Aunt Bertha repeated. Rose was never one for doctors. The treatment would have killed her worse than the cancer.

With the weather warm and the cemetery almost familiar, with all the friends and relatives I'd known all my life, it almost felt like one of the summer parties Hersh and Naomi used to have in the backyard. Even Pearl, the caterer they always used, had been hired to provide the brunch after the unveiling.

Sharon had made the arrangements the way she would have for any other occasion. She'd hired two waitresses and a bartender. Hersh wanted everything to be done exactly the way Naomi would have done it. Sharon insisted she'd do it her own way or not at all. She couldn't see what we'd all noticed, her way was so close to Naomi's it was almost eerie.

Billy, Michael and I stood together near the grave. The stone lay flush to the ground. Hersh had already told us what it would say. Weekly he'd called each of us to report on how he was doing, to tell us what he was eating for dinner, to inform us about ordering the stone. I'm ordering the stone, he'd say, what should I put on it?

You decide, I'd tell him.

Of course I'll decide, he'd say, I'm just asking for an opinion, for crissakes. Lately his temper flashed more fiercely. It cooled quicker, too; then it flared up again. I'd begun to dread his calls.

And by the way, he'd tell me, I'm ordering my own stone, too. And each time it made me sorry I'd been in a hurry to get him off the phone. I'm ordering the stone now, so you won't have to. No one should have to do this.

Thank you, I'd say. Or, Don't be silly, or What's the rush?

When they call to sell us insurance, I told Michael, when the man wants to come and sell us joint cemetery plots, please, I said, tell them no.

What I love, Michael said, is that interesting way you've got of linking marriage to death. My fortieth birthday's around the corner and down the block—if you could lighten up a little, it would help.

The sun kept getting stronger, we were starting to sweat. Billy juggled M&M's in his pocket and popped them three at a time in his mouth.

"Maybe I'll go back to smoking," he said. "It's either that or running. Otherwise, when Cheryl comes back she'll throw me out." He'd grown his beard again, and with the extra weight he was starting to look too solid to be mistaken for a kid anymore.

Prosperous, Grim said, the last time he saw him. You look prosperous. Maybe even successful. You wear it well. All those good reviews must have gone to your head.

For Billy, it was almost as good as having Hersh finally acknowledge he'd grown up, but Hersh was more distracted than ever. His memory bad, his hearing worse, the details of his own life were the only ones that interested him, and even those he could only keep track of if he made a list. And Billy was shy about telling us how well he was doing. He still had a hard time getting used to the idea that he was making money.

One of his singers hit it big, got a standing offer from a good club, signed on for a tour, she had a contract to do two albums. She'd asked Billy to be her musical director and paid him enough money so he could quit his other jobs and still come out ahead. Cheryl took it hard. She said she'd need a year or two to get her own career up to speed. She'd never suspected she'd feel so competitive, but there it was. Billy had changed, so now she'd have to do some changing, too.

They got married in New York on a Friday; Saturday morning she left for Michigan to start graduate school. They saw each other weekends when they could; her Christmas vacation, he'd be on tour in Germany. But at least, they both said, if they were married, they knew she'd come back.

Of all the half-assed things you have done, Sharon said to Billy at the wedding, this is by far the most absurd.

Thank you, Billy said. I know we'll be very happy, too.

Whatever works, Grim said, and rubbed Lonnie's round belly.

Hersh couldn't quite understand Billy and Cheryl's arrangement. More *mishegoss*, he said. Naomi had left him alone with four children he'd never known how to handle. He thought they were grown and gone, but they kept on doing things that seemed to need his supervision and he didn't know what he was supposed to do.

What's the hurry to get married? he said to Billy right before the ceremony. Carol isn't pregnant, is she?

Cheryl, Billy said, and no, she's not.

Of course she's not, Sharon said. With Bill it's always approach avoidance. If he's like that in bed, she'll never get pregnant.

Cheryl tossed Michael the bouquet. You've got to be as crazy as I am to want to get mixed up in this.

I thought, Michael said, we were the ones who were normal. Bringing sanity to this primitive clan.

Don't count on it, Peter said. Lonnie just smiled. Michael insisted we spend the rest of the weekend with Billy after Cheryl left, so he wouldn't have to honeymoon alone.

Cheryl couldn't get to the cemetery in time for the service, she would have flown in later in the day, but Billy had a gig and couldn't stay. They'd see each other in a month.

"I don't know what the big deal is about marriage," Billy said, "it's like falling off a log."

Michael looked at me. "I can see you thinking," he said. "I can actually see the wheels turning as you run it through. It's like falling off a log, cracking your head open on a rock, gasping for air, and then drowning. Am I right?"

I wasn't sure whether or not to tell him he was close, but then I saw Molly arrive, hand in hand with David Werfel.

Hersh hugged her and kissed her and shook hands with David so warmly, even Sharon had to look away.

"I forgot to tell you," Billy said.

"It's a great idea," I said. "I'm surprised Naomi didn't think of it." I tried to get the mud off my left heel. I thought I was smiling, I meant to be cheerful.

Michael put his index finger below my chin and lifted my face; I couldn't avoid looking at him.

"Just so I know," he said. "It really doesn't matter if you did. But did you?"

"No," I said. "Not even close. I never even thought about it. We're just old friends." I'd never asked Michael to account for those six months we'd spent apart. Most of the time he knew better than to ask me.

"Hey, you guys," Molly said, letting go of David's hand to flash a diamond ring at us. "Guess what I caught?" David winked at me. "A real live Jewish doctor. The genuine article. I bet Naomi would have been proud of me."

Sharon stood nearby playing with her pearls, half involved in the conversation going on in her small circle, half involved in the conversation in ours. I pulled her over to our group.

"Molly's getting married, too," I said, drawing her in between Michael and me. "You remember David, don't you?"

She shook his hand. "Vaguely," she said. "You've got something to do with the hospital."

"He's a doctor," Molly said. "A genuine . . ."

Before she could run through it again, David turned her around and walked off toward Grim's group.

"It never would have worked," Michael said. "He was wearing a Rolex and I just can't see you with a guy who's got a Rolex."

"I didn't notice," I said. "No, I mean, you're right—a guy with a Rolex is definitely out of the question."

"The man is history," Billy said.

Oscar was the last of the friends to arrive. He brought his girlfriend Abby, which set The Girls buzzing. Abby at forty-five was too young for him by twenty years at least; he had no business bringing her. But Naomi was the only one who would have had the nerve and the tact to tell him. And Abby, they buzzed, had no business showing up wearing the short mink jacket Oscar had given her, nor was it right for her to be sporting what looked like Helen's cocktail ring.

"He should have known better," Sharon said to me. "He had no business bringing her here. Someone should have told him."

Between Oscar's bringing Abby and Grim bringing the

baby, who was starting to fuss, Sharon was getting more and more upset with the way things were going. Grim passed Nate to Lonnie.

"If she whips out one of those monstrous, ugly breasts right here and starts playing earth mother," Sharon said, speaking loudly enough for both Grim and Lonnie to overhear if they had the good sense to be eavesdropping, "I'm going to ask her to wait in the car." Sharon went to find Hersh to see if she couldn't get him to do something about it.

Peter and the children, another one of Naomi's phrases that stuck, none of us ever referred to them any other way, were perfectly dressed, as usual. And perfectly behaved. They were always so quiet, we sometimes forgot to include them in our conversations. Michael pried his hand loose from mine and went over to talk to them. Billy and I were left alone.

"Well," he said, "I'm feeling a little weird here."

"Me, too," I said. "We don't see enough of you anymore."

"The way Cheryl sees it, even a little bit goes a long way. Listen," he said, and he stepped closer so he could lower his voice, "I wouldn't ask anyone else about this, but do you feel like she's actually here somewhere? This is all so fucking weird, it's not the way I thought it would be."

He picked up a twig and broke it in half, then in half again. "I don't even know if I miss her. It's not as if we saw her all the time. But then sometimes I get the feeling something's different, only I can't figure out what it is." He scooped up three more branches and snapped each one twice before throwing them onto the path between the graves. "Is that how it's supposed to be?"

"I don't know," I said. "I just don't. There are times

when I catch myself doing something right. Something silly like getting dressed and I've really pulled it all together, or cooking dinner and not ruining it, or doing something really smart at work, and I kind of say, See, Naomi, I can take care of myself. And then I wait for a minute because I almost believe she'll say something nice to me."

"I know," he said, "but she never does."

"Not yet," I said.

"Yeah," he said, "she never did before, either."

"Well, children," Hersh said, he put a hand on each of our shoulders. He cleared his throat twice. "As soon as the rest of the family gets here, we'll start. The rabbi said the service should only be about fifteen minutes, then we'll go back to the house." He still needed to go over plans, he still kept lists of what had to be done.

After today, he'd sell the house. After the sale, he'd buy an apartment. After the apartment, he'd go to Florida for a few weeks. After Florida, well, who knows, he'd told each of us a dozen times. Did I tell you I've ordered my own stone so you don't have to worry about it? he'd always ask.

The aunts were late and in a hurry and noisy and full of apologies and getting older. Even without Rose, it still seemed like there were a lot of them. But without Rose, the group didn't hold together as well; they scattered to take places wherever they could, apologizing to people who didn't even know them.

The rabbi took his place by the grave; we'd each been given copies of the prayer we were to say with him, though everyone now knew by heart the words of mourning. Michael stood next to me and held my hand. Billy stood by my other side, he reached for my other hand, then let it drop. I tried to pay attention, but I couldn't keep my eyes on the ground where Naomi was supposed to be buried.

Hersh had tears in his eyes, he kept shaking his head, there's some mistake, he seemed to be saying, this just isn't right. His sisters were crying. Molly was crying, too. The Girls held tissues, a few blew their noses. Oscar cried. Grim, Sharon and Billy were as dry-eyed as I was, they, too, were looking everywhere but at the ground. Then the service was over. Fifteen minutes, as promised. The stone lay exposed. The words said something about the memory of a loving wife and mother. The time between the two dates came to seventy-three. I subtracted them again and I got seventy-two. Either way, it didn't make any difference.

"Now what?" Billy said.

"Life goes on," Aunt Essie told him; she kissed his forehead. "God bless," she said. "May she rest in peace."

"If I had wanted three pitchers of margaritas," Sharon said to the bartender slowly so he'd know just how angry she was, "I would have ordered margaritas. But I did not. I told you specifically Bloody Marys and screwdrivers. If you charge us for the Margaritas, we will not pay."

"Don't start," Hersh said. We were all standing in the den, they'd always had the bar set up in the den when they'd had parties.

Sharon spun around fast to face him. "Don't ever say that to me again," she said.

Billy and I were as startled as Hersh was. She'd changed the script and taken us all into unfamiliar territory. We didn't know how this new scene ended.

Hersh seemed cowed. "All I meant was . . ."

"I'm not interested in what you meant," she said. "Now if you want to take over, that's fine with me. But if you don't," she said and from the way her voice softened to the pitch a mother uses when she's talking to a child, we all knew something serious had irrevocably shifted, "then why don't you take your drink inside and go sit with your company."

Billy and I watched as Hersh obeyed. Even Grim, busy with Nate on his shoulder, saw Hersh grow docile. Grim lifted Nate in the air and held the baby's face close to his, nose to nose. "Someday, kid, you'll turn the tables on me, too. Won't you?"

Nate started to cry and Lonnie leaned over to take him, her blouse already unbuttoned. She sat down in the armchair by the picture window and began feeding the baby.

"This isn't the place," Sharon said. "If you must do that, you can go upstairs to one of our bedrooms."

Lonnie started to get up, but Grim pressed his hand to her shoulder and wouldn't let her. "She's fine right where she is," he said.

"I refuse to let that go on in this house in front of company," Sharon said.

"It's my house as much as it's yours," Grim said. "But the truth is, it doesn't belong to any of us."

As people found their way to the bar and saw we were in the middle of what Naomi would have called making a scene, they quickly got their drinks and left.

"Really, Charlie," Lonnie said, "it's fine. I'll go upstairs. All this fighting is upsetting Nate, anyway."

"Because he's got no business being here in the first place," Sharon said.

"It's the same," Billy said to me, "and it's different. I never thought I'd say this, but at least when Naomi said those things, she had a sense of humor. Maybe sense of humor's too strong for what she had. I don't ever think of her as being very funny. But she had a sense of something. Sharon's so damn serious. God, I need a drink."

Nate didn't look at all upset, he was making those peaceful humming sounds that made everyone but Sharon smile.

Michael had gone to find Peter, thinking that Peter could persuade Sharon to back down. But Peter had even less influence than usual. Sharon was on a roll.

"What are you so uptight about, anyway?" Grim said.

"Women aren't cows," she said.

"No," Grim said, "but some of them sure are bitches."

Billy had gotten the bartender to sneak him a margarita, he'd downed it quickly and was working on a second one. "Let's put it to a vote," he said. "How many people here think Sharon qualifies as a first-rate bitch?"

He raised his hand. He looked to me for agreement.

"Let's drop it," I said.

"There you go again, Saint Beth. Still waiting for someone to pin a gold star on you for being nice. Just once try saying out loud what you like and what you don't. Just try it, please. You'll feel better. I promise."

At first he'd sounded nasty, then he'd sounded nice, confusing me the way Hersh used to with his temper running hot and cold. And it made me cry the way it used to, though I wasn't ever sure why.

Grim was the one to take my side, another shift, another jolt.

"Leave it alone," he said to Billy. "Back off," he said to Sharon. They both grew quiet. He was, after all, the eldest.

"Tomato juice, plain," Aunt Essie told the bartender. "You pour it for me straight from the can. Let me see the can so I know. If it's got anything in it, I get heartburn. At my age, that's all I need. Then I'm in the bathroom all night and I can't sleep."

The bartender had to go into the kitchen to get Aunt

Essie her can of tomato juice. Her eyes were so bad and her balance so shaky, it took her several minutes to turn herself around and see the seven of us in the den. When she spotted Nate on Lonnie's lap, she inched her way over.

"Oh, the baby," she said. "Thank God for the baby. There should always be a baby around when there's a death. It's good luck." She kissed Nate's head, hardly needing to bend down to reach him.

"You're so busy with your indigestion and the baby, you don't even notice our Bethie's crying," Aunt Bertha said. "What is it, darling, you miss your mother?"

The room was getting crowded, though Michael and Peter had just left and Lonnie was making her way toward the door. I was hoping to slip out quietly.

"I'm fine," I said. "It's just a little upsetting, that's all."

"And why not?" Essie said, as I let her cup my chin and pinch my cheeks. "Of course I knew she was upset," she told Bertha. "I just didn't want to upset her anymore by mentioning it."

"I wonder," Bertha said, to no one in particular, "what Hersh is going to do with all these lovely things when he sells the house. She had some very good pieces, you know."

"We'll take care of it," Sharon said. She'd been the one who'd gone through Naomi's personal items, dividing them up fairly, she said. Packing and shipping them to each of us because she knew, she said, exactly what Naomi would have wanted us to get. I'd been so happy to have someone else take care of it, I didn't question her judgment. Billy and Grim both said they didn't care, Lonnie and Cheryl felt they had no right to any of it.

"I've always had my eye on that silver coffeepot," Aunt Bertha said. "Your mother knew how much I loved that."

I left Sharon explaining who was going to get the samovar, who would get the silver tea service. The final decision, she told them, would really be up to Hersh.

In the dining room, at the buffet table, Oscar grabbed me around the waist. "That's what I like," he said. His breath smelled of whiskey and herring. "I want to introduce you to someone." He ran his arm up and down my back as he guided me over to the corner where Abby sat.

Abby was the only one who still had her fur jacket draped over her shoulders, the rest of the furs were piled up on Hersh and Naomi's beds the way they always were for a party. Abby, still new to all this, didn't understand the routine. She wore the jacket and she stayed on the men's side of the room. She let Oscar bring her food, instead of the other way round. She didn't know the caterer's name. And that definitely was Helen's ring she wore. I'd heard The Girls talking, it was only a partial list of her sins. There was more, but they'd lowered their voices and I'd missed the rest. Abby was a year younger than Grim.

"Your father should only be so lucky," Oscar said. "I keep trying to get him to go out with us, but he won't go. Abby has a friend, a wonderful girl. But he just stays home. You talk to him," he said. "He'll listen."

"I'm not so sure," I said. "He never has before."

"I'm worried about him," Oscar said. "I wouldn't mention it if I didn't think it was serious. You know me, I don't go where I'm not wanted. But he needs to get out. It's a seller's market out there. The women are desperate for us. He doesn't like young, he could have old. He could have invitations every night of the week. Talk to him."

Abby held out her empty glass. "See if they can't make this one with Absolut," she said. "I can't believe they don't have any."

Michael would have urged me to stay out of it, but Michael wasn't around. I went off to find Hersh; I didn't like the idea of his sitting home alone every night.

He wasn't in the dining room with his friends, he wasn't in the living room with his family. The kitchen, the den, the front hall were crowded with people, but he wasn't there. I found him upstairs in his room, sitting on the edge of his bed. He kept Naomi's bed made. He had the housekeeper change the sheets on both beds every week.

I hadn't expected him to be there, so I'd gone in even though the door was closed. He was talking on the phone.

"Sevenish," he said into the receiver and then hung up quickly.

"You all right?" he said to me.

"I'm fine," I said, "I was just coming up to ask you the same thing."

"You don't have to worry about me, if that's what you're thinking." He played with the switch for the electric blanket. Once when Naomi was in the hospital, he'd taken a box of chocolates to bed with him. He fell asleep with the blanket turned up high, when he woke up, his pillow was resting in a pool of melted chocolate and caramel. Ever since he'd kept constant watch on the blanket control.

"Good," I said. "I'm glad I don't." Talking to him was easier now that he'd started wearing his hearing aid all the time.

"I would have told you about her," he said, looking down at the telephone. "But what would I say? I'm not going to marry her. She's just company. I get lonely."

"I know you do," I said. "You should be going out."

"It's been a year," he said.

"Almost a year," I said. Roz had told me it would take two years for us to recover. Two years, she said. We'd probably all make too many changes and be more susceptible to colds. She advised me to increase my daily dose of vitamin C. I'd passed the idea on to Hersh on the off chance that she was right. He had a bottle of vitamin C, along with a bottle of Maalox, on his night table.

"What am I doing? I'm too old for this," he said. "Your mother would say I'm an old goat and she's only interested in money."

"No, she'd probably want you to be happy."

"Since when?" he said. "Did I already tell you I'm going to sell the house and take an apartment?"

"Would someone please go downstairs," Sharon said, walking right into the middle of the room and glaring at Hersh, "and explain to Oscar that this is not a party, that we do not have to serve every kind of drink his little tart wants."

"This," Hersh said, "I will handle my way."

He stood up and kissed me. "I'm all right," he said. "You just take care of yourself."

Michael and Peter were in my room looking through my old records. Michael picked an ancient Bob Dylan album and put it on the record player I'd gotten for my sixteenth birthday. Peter sat on the floor and leaned against the wall. He drank from a silver flask, he held my old teddy bear on his lap.

"Now that you've found us," Peter said, "please don't ask us to go back downstairs."

I flopped down on my bed and gave Michael what I hoped by now he understood was my what's-going-on-here look. Michael looked back with an expression I was sure meant, later.

"That isn't really music," Billy said. He'd come up to

say goodbye. "Not even close to music," he said the way he always did when I'd listen to Dylan. Up until now, it was our only major disagreement.

"We'll talk this week," he said to me. "We'll straighten it out. I really didn't mean to hurt you."

"Maybe you kind of did," I said. "Something's changed, it'll just take us a while to get used to it."

"Well, let's hurry it up, then," he said. "I miss you. If I can't get there sooner, I'll be down for the wedding."

"You better be," I said. "I couldn't get through it without you."

When he smiled, I noticed for the first time he'd had the gap between his teeth filled in.

He said he was going, but then he sat down on the floor with Peter and Michael and stayed. I said we really ought to go back downstairs; everyone agreed, but nobody moved. Michael switched from Bob Dylan to Johnny Mathis; Billy groaned and pretended to be in pain. Peter, who looked what Naomi would have called three sheets to the wind, said, "This reminds me, Sharon and I are separated."

"What?" I said. "She never mentioned it."

"I moved out two days ago."

"Then you could move back," I said.

"No," he said. "I can't. I only came with her today because I'd promised the kids. But after this, it's over."

I looked at Michael again, and Michael gave me his leave-it-alone, I'll-tell-you-about-it-later look.

"I can't blame you," Billy said. He looked a little looped. "But isn't there some way you can work it out so you get to stay part of this family and she doesn't?"

" 'Fraid not," Peter said. "I would have left sooner, but I didn't want to upset your mother. Then I thought I ought to give Sharon some time to get over her death. The other night she told me she'd been thinking about leaving me for years. She just wasn't sure I could handle it. 'I'm the one who's leaving,' I said. 'No, you're not,' she said, 'I am.' "

"Yeah," Billy said, "that sounds like Sharon."

"I'm sorry," I said, "you always seemed like such a perfect couple."

"Is that a compliment?" Billy said.

Molly and David poked their heads in the doorway. "Your dad said we'd find you here." Molly was wearing a black silk scarf that used to be Naomi's. Hersh had made Sharon include Molly when she divided up Naomi's things.

Michael looked at me once when David sat down next to me, then he deliberately looked away and wouldn't look back. Molly joined the group on the floor.

"He seems like a nice guy," David said.

"He really is," I said. I looked to see if Michael was listening, but he was busy picking out records.

"Maybe next time," David said. And I checked to make sure Michael was still busy.

"Okay, you two," Molly said. She'd finished saying goodbye to Peter, Michael and Billy. "You had your chance and you blew it. Now, just wish each other luck and let's get on with it."

"Well, if you didn't," Michael said, when Molly and David were gone, "then you should have. I think he's still in love with you."

"Never was and never will be," I said. "Now you sound like my mother."

"He doesn't sound like my mother," Billy said.

Grim and Lonnie brought Nate upstairs so he could sleep in Grim's old room. They needed to stay, they said, close enough to hear him when he woke up. I gave Grim and

Lonnie the bed and sat beside Michael on the floor. Billy was still saying he was leaving any minute. Peter's flask was empty and he kept saying he was going to go downstairs and refill it. Michael had replaced Johnny Mathis with Joan Baez, and Lonnie wanted to know who all these singers were.

Sharon passed by with the aunts still taking inventory. She returned alone, carrying a pitcher of margaritas and a stack of plastic glasses.

"It's a shame to waste all this," she said.

"You know sometimes," Billy said, "you're not half bad."

Michael and Peter drank to that.

Everyone was quiet until Billy pulled out the scrapbook Naomi had put together for me when I graduated from high school. Before I could stop him, he set it down in Michael's lap.

"Bet you never saw this," Billy said to him.

"No," I said, "and he doesn't have to now."

"But I'd like to," Michael said and he flipped the book open to the most embarrassing picture of all. The one of me in my first pair of eyeglasses. Eight years old and so mortified I didn't want to go to school. It was Naomi's idea, though I'd been sure it was Mary's, to take a picture of me so I'd see it wasn't all that bad. The idea backfired. When I saw the photograph, I felt even worse. My hair was messy, my knees were chubby, my dress looked silly. The minute I saw the picture, I started to tell Michael all that, but he put his finger to my lips.

"Shh," he said. "Look again," and he put the album in my lap. "Really look this time," he said, and I tried. "There," he said, "is a neat little kid. A great little kid. If we had a kid like that, we'd want a picture of her, too."

"I guess," I said, "she's not that bad."

"Not bad at all," Billy said.

"In fact," Grim said, "she was so goddamn cute, it would have made you sick."

"It was awful," Sharon said.

"But I always thought," I started to say.

"We know what you always thought," Billy said. "But that, as they say, is your problem."

For the first time, Sharon agreed with him. "Low self-esteem," she said.

"A profound lack therof," Grim said. "A nearly cosmic void."

"You were fine," Michael said, "you still are."

"Okay," I said, "now I really am embarrassed." I put the album back on the bookshelf. When Hersh sold the house, I'd probably decide to take it with me, but for the time being it belonged in my room. "I like it better when we pick on someone else."

"Don't we all," Sharon said.

I said it was time to go and Michael was the only one to stand up. We said goodbye to everyone. We said we'd see them in three weeks. We said there was no chance we'd change our minds about the wedding at this point.

Billy said, the way Mary used to, that wild horses couldn't keep him away. And Grim said he'd be there with bells on, an expression as out of character for him as it usually was for Hersh. Peter wished us luck, he was afraid he might have to miss it. Lonnie said she hoped we didn't mind that she'd be bringing the baby. And Sharon said she'd be there, but she'd believe it when she saw it. Which was just exactly what Naomi would have said.